A Pride & Prejudice
Time Travel Romance

Moments *of* Moments Infinite

THE MEMORY SERIES #4

NEY MITCH

Readers, thank you so much for reading this far, and I hope you enjoy the last installment of this series. I hope that the choices made will be a satisfying conclusion for you and therefore I dedicate this book to you for partaking in the last bit of this journey.

Chapter One

OF COURSE!

T he moment continued with a series of stares.

I stared at Lady Catherine in disdain, still holding my face from where she had slapped me.

She looked at me as if I was an ant that she wished to crush under her shoe.

Darcy looked at her as well.

And everyone else in the room was looking at me!

Then Darcy and I turned to each other.

"I'm engaged?" Darcy asked me.

"Why the devil are you asking her if you are engaged?" Lady Catherine bellowed. "You very well know that you are."

Then Earl Fitzwilliam came forward.

"Oh, for goodness sakes, Catherine!" Earl Fitzwilliam said. "First, I will not have that behavior in my home, so you will desist immediately. And second, you know that is not valid."

"Of course, it is valid," Lady Catherine cried. "It is ironclad as if Darcy here had scribbled his signature on the wedding papers. Is that not so, Fitzwilliam?"

"But—" Darcy began, and then he closed his mouth and so I decided to do what he loved best: let me speak for him.

"If he is engaged to your daughter, then where has she been for the last few months?" I asked. "For in the time I have known Darcy, he has spoken not a word about her, and I doubt that if he were to be engaged, he would forget that he had a fiancée."

"Well, he does have one."

"And yet it sounds like he doesn't."

"Truly, it sounds like I don't," Darcy added, "for where is my fiancée?"

"Where you left her," Lady Catherine argued. "At her home, Rosings Park."

"Then why aren't we married yet?"

"Because you are taking a long time."

"I wonder why that is," he replied, sarcastic.

"Catherine," Lady Fitzwilliam interrupted, "this is not the time to do this now."

"Thank you, Lady Fitzwilliam," Aunt Gardiner said, stepping near me, protective, "but I am wondering, Lady Catherine. Your daughter is not here with you to fight for her fiancé, yet you are here claiming something that Mr. Darcy does not know of. Then you lay violent hands on my niece, and you think yourself justified to do it. I will not stand for this."

"And nor shall I," Lady Catherine replied, turning back to Darcy. "You are engaged to my daughter, now what have you to say?"

"He need not say anything," I interrupted, "for only that if he were engaged to her, then he would not have made an offer to me."

"Their engagement is of a peculiar kind. They have been attached to one another, intended for one another, since their infancy."

"Are you speaking of an arranged marriage?" Kitty gasped. "Is that what that means?"

"Yes, it does," Colonel Fitzwilliam answered with a sigh. "Aunt Catherine, you planned their marriage, and not they themselves."

"It was every day implied, just never fully declared. It was the dearest wish of your mother, Darcy, and of me."

"But not of me, then?" Darcy refuted. "You're telling me that I've been engaged to a woman since before I could even walk? All because you and my mother wanted it?"

"It was her dearest wish! Do you now think yourself so proud, and in fact are so inconsiderate that you forget what she wanted?"

"If she loved me, then she would not have ordered me around in that way."

"Besides," Aunt Gardiner continued, "by the sounds of it, your schemes and machinations are simply the results of two women being romantic when they became mothers. I have children myself, madam, and I know the way our minds work. We wish for them to grow up and become the best or marry the best. Could it be that you had the best example in front of you, when Mr. Darcy's late mother had a child around the time you did, your imaginations ran wild, and now you slap my niece all because your dreams did not come true?"

"Precisely," Mary supported. "Your resolutions seem to be the work of a mind being fanciful, and no more."

"It was true! Darcy, you are engaged to Anne, and that is final."

"Aunt, please…" Zachary Fitzwilliam sighed.

"No, I will be heard."

"Miss Bennet," replied her ladyship, looking back to me, "you ought to know, that I am not to be trifled with. But however insincere *you* may choose to be, you shall not find *me* so. My character has ever been celebrated for its sincerity and frankness, and in a cause of such moment as this, I shall certainly not depart from it."

She took a deep breath, which made her jowls wobble. "My nephew is already engaged to my daughter. While in their cradles, his mother and I planned the union, and now, at the moment when the wishes of both sisters would be accomplished in their marriage, to be prevented by a young woman of inferior birth, of no importance in the world, and wholly unallied to the family!

"Do you pay no regard to the wishes of his friends? To his tacit engagement with Miss de Bourgh? Are you lost to every feeling of propriety and delicacy? Have you not heard me say that from his earliest hours he was destined for his cousin?" High color rose in her normally pallid cheeks.

"If he were destined for his cousin, then he would not make an offer to me," I countered.

"It ought to be so. It must be so, while he retains the use of his reason. But your arts and allurements may, in a moment of infatuation, have made him forget what he owes to himself and to all his family. You may have drawn him in."

I stood firm. "If I have, I shall be the last person to confess it."

"Miss Bennet, do you know who I am? I am not accustomed to such language as this. I am almost the nearest relation he has in the world and am entitled to know all his dearest concerns."

"But you are not entitled to know mine, nor will such behavior as this, ever induce me to be explicit."

3

She poked an arthritic finger at me. "Let me be rightly understood. This match, to which you have the presumption to aspire, can never take place."

"But it has taken place," Jane answered for me, and I was surprised at how firm she sounded, for indeed, she had never done so before. "And that will not be denied, nor shall it be. My sister is engaged to your nephew, and I will not allow you to trouble her any further. You have laid violent hands on my sister, and I will not allow it.

"I am Jane Bennet, the eldest daughter of Longbourn, and I have four sisters whom I care for deeply. So, this I say, and this I vow. You will cease and desist from any verbal attacks on her, you will apologize for your disturbing behavior which is very much unlike how any great lady should act, and then you shall quit this house immediately. However, if you continue in this manner, then I can assure you, lay one more hand on her, and I will... I will..." Her color was high and her eyes blazing. "I will throw you out that window with extreme enthusiasm!"

Lady Catherine looked at Jane in shock, as did all of us.

"Oh, Jane." I sighed, half-smiling, but I could not say more for I was very much in awe. Lady Catherine then turned to my sister, flushed and red in the face.

"What did you say to me?"

"What any older sister would say to the woman who slapped her sister for no reason."

Lady Catherine turned back to me.

"And you still have not apologized for your disgusting display of violence upon her," Mary added. "We are waiting for your words of repentance."

Lady Catherine ignored her. "Miss Elizabeth, you will hear me."

"Yes, and I had heard it before. But what is that to me? If there is no other objection to my marrying your nephew, I shall certainly not be kept from it by knowing that his mother and aunt wished him to marry Miss de Bourgh. You both did as much as you could in planning the marriage. Its completion depended on others. If Mr. Darcy is neither by honor nor inclination confined to his cousin, why is not he to make another choice? And if I am that choice, why may not I accept him?"

"Because honor, decorum, prudence, nay, interest, forbid it. Yes, Miss Bennet, interest, for do not expect to be noticed by his family or friends, if you willfully act against the inclinations of all. You will be censured, slighted, and despised, by everyone connected with him. Your alliance will be a disgrace; your name will never even be mentioned by any of us."

"These are heavy misfortunes, but the wife of Mr. Darcy must have such extraordinary sources of happiness necessarily attached to her situation, that she could, upon the whole, have no cause to repine."

"Obstinate, headstrong girl! I am ashamed of you! You are to understand, Miss Elizabeth, that I came here with the determined resolution of carrying my purpose, nor will I be dissuaded from it. I have not been used to submit to any person's whims."

She paced back and forth. "I have not been in the habit of brooking disappointment. My daughter and my nephew are formed for each other. They are descended, on the maternal side, from the same noble line; and, on the father's, from respectable, honorable, and ancient, though untitled, families. Their fortune on both sides is splendid. They are destined for each other by the voice of every member of their respective houses, and what is to divide them? The upstart pretensions of a young woman without family, connections, or fortune."

She whirled around and faced me, her expression grim. "Is this to be endured? But it must not, shall not be. If you were sensible of your own good, you would not wish to quit the sphere in which you have been brought up."

"Lady Catherine," Jane interrupted, "in marrying your nephew, she should not consider herself as quitting that sphere. He is a gentleman; we are a gentleman's daughters. So far we are equal."

"True. You *are* a gentleman's daughter. But who was your mother? Who are your uncles and aunts? Do not imagine me ignorant of their condition."

"We are right here," Uncle Gardiner said, "and we are the working class of London. Never shall I deny this, but my trade has given me wealth and as much consequence in the world as many in the landed gentry. Therefore what is occurring, Lady Catherine, but the beginning of a great change, where you and your pride shall give way to us who are new and whom you need. The society of our country is bought by the labor of others; therefore to look down at my nieces because of us is futile and foolish."

"And whatever my connections may be," I argued, "if your nephew does not object to them, they can be nothing to *you*. You wish of us not to be married, you have stated this eight times at least since you have entered your brother's home. But I am not to be intimidated into anything so wholly unreasonable. Your ladyship wants Mr. Darcy to marry your daughter, but would my giving you the wished-for promise make their marriage at all more probable?"

I linked my arm through Darcy's. "Supposing him to be attached to me, would my refusing to accept his hand make him wish to bestow it on his cousin? Allow me to say, Lady Catherine, that the arguments with which you have supported this extraordinary application have been as frivolous as the application was ill-judged. You have widely mistaken my character, if you think I can be worked on by such persuasions as these. And I believe that you have mistaken your nephew as well. But you have certainly no right to concern yourself in mine. I must beg, therefore, to be importuned no farther on the subject."

"But—"

"Will you have done, madam!" Kitty protested. "For that is quite enough."

"Quite enough indeed," Jane added. "You have your answer."

"Not so hasty, if you please. I have by no means done. To all the objections I have already urged, I have still another to add. I am no stranger to the particulars of your youngest sister's infamous elopement. And she is here now, isn't she?"

Instinctively, we all turned to Lydia, who flinched.

⚜

"Ah." Lady Catherine smiled wickedly. "Yes, it is you then, is it not?"

Lydia looked down for a second and we all buckled under the weight of the truth. Yet Lady Catherine, who had been saving this all for the opportune moment, felt our resolve weakening as she had reached an ideal point in the argument, a chink in our armor, if that was the correct term for it. This would weaken us, invariably, and she was prepared to win due to it.

"I know it all," Lady Catherine boomed, then turned to Earl and Lady Fitzwilliam. "And now it is time that you did. For when you do, you shall have this family removed from your home, and see them as nothing short of a tumor on Matlock's side that ought to be removed. I heard it all, from my reverend at Hunsford, Mr. William Collins, who is their cousin."

I closed my eyes at this news, for all things considered, we had for a brief time, believed the scandal to be quite over and done with, but the world was too small, too miniscule for the shame to disappear. At least where men such as Mr. Collins were involved.

Of course he would be the reverend to Lady Catherine.

Of course he would be our cousin.

Of course he would propose to Mary, and then drop her at the merest hint of the word 'scandal'.

And of course he would tell Lady Catherine, not feeling any remorse or sensitivity to the woman he once was engaged to.

We had never outraced the scandal, but rather we had only postponed the result of it.

"Lady Catherine," Mary interrupted, "I offer advice of you exercising moderation. There are some things that you need to allow someone to leave in their own past."

Lady Catherine ignored her and continued.

"This creature," Lady Catherine said, pointing her walking stick at Lydia, "has a sordid history that is meant for the worst of gossip columns in the papers, making her the worst woman to be mistress of Matlock. Indeed, I know not what you were thinking, Zachary!"

"She loves me!" Zachary thundered.

"She loves that she can use you to hide that she is no longer a maid!"

"What?" Earl Fitzwilliam said, turning to Lydia.

"Yes, all true it is!" Lady Catherine bellowed. "This selfish girl, hedonistic to a fault, eloped with a man, and what man would it be? But the son of the late Mr. Darcy's steward! Mr. George Wickham himself! Yes, she eloped with him to London, where the only reason that she is not married to him is simply because he must not have wanted her."

"That is not true!" I declared.

"Which part of it? The elopement part or the whole 'how dare she even show her face here' part? And is such a girl to be my nephew's sister? Heaven and earth! Of what are you thinking? Are the shades of Matlock to be thus polluted?"

"You can now have nothing further to say," Jane resentfully answered. "You have insulted my sisters in every possible method. I threatened you once, and I hold to it still."

"And this one has the impertinence to threaten me!"

"You struck her sister and insulted the rest," Aunt Gardiner cried.

"Wait!" Earl Fitzwilliam shouted, and we all turned to him. "What is this business of an elopement?"

When he asked this, we all kept our mouths closed, all but Lady Catherine of course!

"Indeed, Miss Lydia, how can you account for it yourself? Tell us, am I lying, because I have it on good account. Try and lie, I beg of you." She looked down her pointed nose at my sister, her eyes angry and forbidding.

"Lydia," Jane said, "it is fine, you do not have to—"

"But I must," Lydia said. "Thank you, Jane, but I must. Or perhaps, I ought to."

"Yes, you ought to," Lady Catherine said, and then she turned to Darcy. "And now you shall see the sort of people that you shall gain by agreeing to a connection with this sordid family."

"I know the connections that I am gaining, aunt," Darcy replied stubbornly, taking my hand, "and I shall not waver now."

Lady Catherine turned to me, venomous.

"What did you do to him!"

"I accepted the man he was, rather than what you have done."

"Enough," Lydia declared, then she turned to Earl and Lady Fitzwilliam. "I wish not to have everything fall apart because of me but being honest is a virtue on its own. Ask me of my past, and I shall tell you everything."

Chapter Two

THE CONFESSION OF LYDIA BENNET

"Yet I will not have my sisters lose the respect of those in this room," Lydia said sternly. "I have made a mistake; these are my actions and mine alone. My family shall not suffer for it."

"Your family is your family," Lady Catherine stated bluntly.

"But every soul is his or her own," Lydia said wisely, "and ought not to carry the blame of others. I made a mistake, and no one will suffer for it but me."

Lydia then turned to the Fitzwilliams and faced them. "Earl and Lady Fitzwilliam, I thank you very much for inviting me to your home and being content in your son's choice of me. Yet what Lady Catherine said is correct, for I had indeed, in my past, eloped with Mr. George Wickham, believing that we would marry."

Earl and Lady Fitzwilliam looked at each other, alarmed.

"This is not long past," Lady Catherine interjected, "but only mere months ago."

"I believed that I was in love."

"That is always the excuse!"

"I thought we were going to marry!"

"And once more, that is always the excuse. An elopement is scandalous and horrible. Only the very worst woman would even think of indulging the idea of it."

"Label me as you wish," Lydia said, "but you all see that I am not married to him, so the engagement did not come to fruition."

"Because he rejected you."

"I also rejected him!" Lydia shouted. "I discovered that he was the worst of men, I did not run from this fact, force him to marry me, or even ask my family to pay him off and bribe him into marrying me. No, indeed, I did not. When I realized that he was using me, that I was in error and was a fool for my actions, I sought to rectify them, risking the ridicule of the world than attach myself to what I saw was a foolish desire."

She glanced at the floor and rubbed her arms. "I made a mistake, and it hurt many. I am not perfect, never have been, nor shall I ever be. In fact, I am broken, and I am…not a maid. Yet my mistakes have educated me. In fact, I have learned more in these last couple of months than I have learned in the course of my life. Within me, there is much room for improvement. Much room for humility. Indeed, I have a past that is not ideal, but I love your son. I shall improve with him at my side."

Earl and Lady Fitzwilliam were silent for a moment, but the Earl shook his head.

"I cannot allow this," the Earl said at last. "I cannot allow you to marry my son."

Lydia's lips trembled.

"Father…" Zachary began.

"Do not argue with me!" Earl Fitzwilliam shouted. "I am an Earl, and this cannot be so. A mistress with such a repulsive nature! And deceitful, for she has lied to you."

"She never lied to me."

"Yes she did, for she never told you of this—"

"She did," Zachery interrupted.

Lady Fitzwilliam's mouth dropped open. "You knew?"

"Yes, I knew," he answered. "Lydia here told me when I proposed. Why do you think I am willing to marry her?"

"You're willing to marry a woman who did this?"

"Yes, for she was honest with me and gave me a choice. She never deceived me and pretended she was what she was not. Lydia could have not told me, but she did. She respected me enough to choose if I still wished for her rather than if I did not. How could I deny her, when she showed me that she was trustworthy and would always be honest with me?"

"Honest with you." Lady Catherine nearly snorted. "She eloped with another man."

"She told me!"

"And this is good enough for you?" Lady Catherine asked. "By this calculation, you admire her for this?"

"None of us is perfect, Aunt. Myself included."

"You are an earl's son and heir; you cannot marry her!"

"He can and he shall," Lydia hissed, "for I love him deeply, if his parents permit."

"Which I cannot do," Lady Fitzwilliam said, standing up. "For Zachary, this is not what we had planned for you."

"I know the feeling."

"I love your son," Lydia said. "But I shall not tear this family apart."

"I have an inheritance," Zachary magnified.

"That can be removed from you, posthaste," Earl Fitzwilliam countered.

"It cannot and you know it," Colonel Fitzwilliam said, "for you have tried."

"And would happiness be so little?" Zachary continued. "When Lydia has behaved nothing short of admirably and I have not been a saint myself. In perspective of the women in the room, I have had my share of dalliances. What makes me better? Or worse? No, I will marry Lydia."

"And I wish to have your blessing," Lydia said, "for I wish to marry him. More than anything." She hooked her arm through his and looked up into his eyes. "And I will marry him, for I will fight for him."

"Our family cannot invite a scandal," Lady Fitzwilliam pointed out.

"Scandals fade over time," I said. "For the sting of it is quite diminishing already."

"But I cannot allow it," Lady Catherine cried. "Remove them from the house, brother, for you must not have the good name of Fitzwilliam and the shades of Matlock be polluted with such a family."

"It is already polluted with such a family," Georgiana whispered, just loud enough for all to hear.

"But it is not too late for it to be remedied."

"It is, for it was always here, with me."

"Georgiana," I interrupted, "you do not have to do this."

"But I must. If it leads to Fitz getting married as he wishes, then you know that I must." Georgiana turned to Lady Catherine and prepared herself. "Aunt Catherine, you cannot turn Lydia away for her previous mistakes, because her past is one that we share."

"Pardon?" Lady Fitzwilliam said.

"Indeed, I am in earnest. Lydia underwent an elopement. And so have I." Georgiana went over her history with Mr. Wickham, and as she spoke, all were silent. When she finished, she turned to the rest of us. "Am I to be disregarded, cast out because of this?" she asked. "For I had made the same mistake."

She turned to Lady Catherine, who was flabbergasted. She gasped and put her bony hand over her mouth. "Georgiana, it cannot be true."

Georgiana stood tall. "But it can, because it is."

"Oh, dear me, Georgiana," Aunt Fitzwilliam said, wringing her hands.

"Thank you, Miss Darcy," Lydia said softly, "thank you ever so much."

"You're welcome, but I could not in good conscience remain here and be silent all throughout your banishment and allow it. I'd be damned for all time if I was, and my immortal soul concerns me as much as my mortal one."

"And to clarify," Darcy stated, "I will brook no offensive words spoken against my sister. She was young and believed herself to be in love. People have gone farther in the name of the emotion, so she will not be blamed for it. Only Mr. Wickham and his damned powers of persuasion ought to be so. Georgiana is quite guiltless, and she does this out of the goodness of her heart, and a large heart it is."

"Yet still, you did not elope, and that made all the difference in the world," Lady Catherine argued.

"I did not elope because Fitzwilliam was there to save me just in time, and of no actions of my own," Georgiana elaborated. "This you know, and this you cannot deny. Therefore, if you cast out Lydia now, and the Bennets, then you are casting them out for something that I myself had planned to do. The only excuse that you have is that I am family, yet therein would lead to hypocrisy of the highest order, for you extend one set of rules for your family and another set for those who are not. Is this what we are?"

Georgiana took a step forward to her Aunt and Uncle Fitzwilliam.

"Mr. Wickham is—persuasive. He is very charming. Always has been and always shall be. It hurts me to even speak of it. But Lydia and I were young when we did this. Lydia still is young. And therefore, are we not to be pitied? Are we to be handed over to the contempt of the world for youthful folly?"

We all turned to Lady Catherine, who had been silent the whole time.

"Well, Aunt," Darcy said, with no feeling or empathy toward her, for he had only met her recently, "will you accept my fiancée, for she shall be my wife, and I will have no other. Or will you not?"

Lady Catherine turned to me once more.

"You have no regard, then, for the honor and credit of my nephew! Unfeeling, selfish girl! Do you not consider that a connection with you must disgrace him in the eyes of everybody?"

"Lady Catherine, I have nothing further to say. You know my sentiments," I added.

"You are then resolved to have him?"

"I am."

"And for god sakes, Aunt," Darcy groaned, "will you stop talking about me right in front of me!"

"I cannot because you have quite forgotten yourself, Darcy. Indeed, you are not the nephew that I helped raise! That I thought was perfect for my daughter. Yet all you need is some of the memory to return to you. Come with me to Rosings Park. See Anne once more and you shall remember who you were and what you owe to your family."

"I only owe myself my own happiness, and not care about those who do not take that into account."

"You refuse, then, to oblige me. You refuse to obey the claims of duty, honor, and gratitude." She turned to me. "You are determined to ruin him in the opinion of all his friends and make him the contempt of the world."

"Neither duty, nor honor, nor gratitude," I continued, "have any possible claim on me, in the present instance. No principle of either would be violated by my marriage with Mr. Darcy. And with regard to the resentment of his family, or the indignation of the world, if the former *were* excited by his marrying me, it would not give me one moment's concern, and the world in general would have too much sense to join in the scorn."

"And this is your real opinion! This is your final resolve! Very well. I shall now know how to act. Do not imagine, Miss Bennet", she vowed, shaking a crooked finger at me, "that your ambition will ever be gratified. I came to try you. I hoped to find you reasonable."

Jane stepped forward. "Very well, now I am about to throw you out of the window."

All gasped as Jane halted just a few steps away from Lady Catherine. Her hands were on her hips. "That was the last warning, madam."

"And you!" Lady Catherine cried. "I thought you refined and genteel, and once more, you Bennets are not what you seem, for you lack any sort of grace and are crass."

"What I am is correcting your error of coming here and offending all. I have no loyalty to you, madam, and owe you nothing. The only things that are of my concern is my future husband, my sisters, and Miss Darcy, who you just offended by attacking my sister, Lydia. I am doing as I see fit, and what I see fit is what I do now. This is the last word you shall have. Use it wisely. Will you accept my sister, pardon my other sister's history, never offend Georgiana again, or will you not?"

Lady Catherine's jaw grew tight and then she turned to crossness once more.

"I take no leave of you, Miss Bennet and your sisters! I send no compliments to your mother. You deserve no such attention. I am most seriously displeased and have never been thus treated in my entire life."

She then turned to Earl and Lady Fitzwilliam.

"I shall return soon, so be prepared for us."

"Us, Catherine?" Earl Fitzwilliam said. "What do you mean by us?"

But Lady Catherine was no longer attentive and was already proceeding out of the room where she ordered the servants to bring her carriage around.

Lady Fitzwilliam followed her, but all was over and done with very quickly, and Lady Catherine had quite left Matlock.

Eventually Lady Fitzwilliam returned.

She heaved a great sigh. "Well, we very much have not seen the last of her."

"But I have," Darcy stated solemnly. "She offended my fiancée greatly, and I shall never receive her again."

"Nephew," Earl Fitzwilliam said.

"I want no excuses for her!" Darcy bellowed with such sternness that all dared not refuse him, and it made me admire him even more. "I despise such behavior. And no, I shall not put up with it!"

"Indeed, sir, you should not," Uncle Gardiner confirmed, and it made me even more proud of Darcy.

"Now the question then remains," I said, turning to the Fitzwilliam's sons, "what are your plans for my sisters? Will you relinquish them, or will you remain true to your words and be the gentlemen that we all believe you are?"

"I proposed to your sister, and not to fear of scandal," Colonel Fitzwilliam said, still remaining by Kitty.

"And I already knew what I was getting involved in, and never believed it to be anything else," Zachary said.

"Your sons love us, Earl and Lady Fitzwilliam," Kitty implored them. "And I wish for you to believe that we intend to be the best wives to them, for we did not fall in love with their names, wealth or status. If you do not accept me as your daughter-in-law, then that really shall not stop me from fighting for him regardless."

"As with I," Lydia said. "I have made many mistakes in my life, and now have seen the beauties of stopping. Your son is the reward for me growing into the woman that I ought to have been. Yet if I had not made the mistake I had, then would I appreciate him now? I know not! Would I even have met him if I had not fallen in some way? I know not the answer to that either. All that I know is that I have never felt this way before."

"But you felt for another man enough to elope with him," Earl Fitzwilliam countered.

"Father," Zachary began, but his father roared over him, silencing Zachary, and then he turned to Lydia.

"You promise that your character has improved?" the Earl asked.

"Yes, I have."

"And you are prepared to be the best woman in the world for my son?" Lady Fitzwilliam asked. "I know that your sister is ideal for my Colonel here, but you are now the only question. My son Zachary is the heir of Matlock and is a great man. You had better be the best of women for him now."

"I shall be," Lydia promised, her gaze not leaving Zachary.

"And understand a mother's love!" Lady Fitzwilliam added. "For if you prove to be anything less than an ideal wife, I have no scruples in causing a scandal and urging him to annul the marriage at any moment. And I will carry my point across, to the very end. The strength of a mother's love, Miss Lydia, now you see it. The strength of a mother's love."

"Mother, she shall be perfect for me," Zachary said.

"I need to hear her swear, though."

"I swear," Lydia promised.

"Do you? Do you understand what that means?"

"I do indeed, and I swear. I love your son. I will marry him, and I will fight to be the best of wives. I cannot guarantee that I shall be the very best of wives, because I do not believe that there is even a true definition of how to be that."

"Now is not the time for jokes."

"I love a good joke, yet in the moment I was being perfectly serious."

Zachary could not help but chuckle at this, and the Earl and Lady Fitzwilliam were left to stand there to ponder.

⚛

Looking from one son to the other, they realized the situation was nothing else but hopeless, for it was what it would always be.

"Very well," Earl Fitzwilliam said at last. "My sons shall have what they wish. For I have seen the horrors of arranged marriages, and I know that to contradict the matter would be foolish. But my sons remember: You have brought this all quite on yourselves."

"Thank you," both sons said in their own way, and all was as it ought to have been, as the confession of Lydia and the strength of Georgiana led to a good outcome.

However temporary that outcome would be.

Chapter Three

THE DESPERATE PLEAS OF AN EARL

That night, Darcy and I lay in bed, after having just made love in the most passionate way that one can and we were quite spent.

"There was urgency to this act of love-making," I noticed. "I wonder at it."

"Love-making can be enhanced due to the actions that preceded it," Darcy informed me. "We both have had a trying day, making our passion for each other increase. That is why this session of intimacy was more intense; we both needed each other after that circumstance."

"My god." I sighed, kissing his chest. "I cannot believe that happened!"

"I both can and can't. After all, when have we ever fully gotten a moment of peace?"

"Oh, upon my word!" I realized. "You are right. First I fall into your world, come between you and your horrible fiancée, then I fall back into my own time, you fall after me right when I am in the middle of a horrible triangle of love, then my sister elopes, then my other sister loses her fiancé, then my other two sisters fall in love with your cousins who are also not your cousins, and now we are here. You have not really had the chance to get bored."

"And now I desire boredom, more than anything else."

"Be careful with what you wish for. Oh, never mind, for that is rubbish. Boredom is precisely what we need right now."

"Yes, it is," he agreed. I am surprised that Zachary is still marrying Lydia though. I did not see that coming."

"For once, a woman was right for being honest. She had told him the truth, and therefore he felt safe. But for the Earl and Lady... I am surprised that they gave in so very easily. I'm even surprised that they supported the match to begin with. My sisters are the last women in the world that an Earl would want his sons to marry, but so it was. How surprising it all is."

We were interrupted by a knock on the door.

I fell out of the bed onto the floor to hide.

"Did you really just fall on the floor?" Darcy laughed as he jumped out and handed me one of his shirts.

I groaned. "Yes, I did. What else was I to do? I was desperate!"

"Clearly," Darcy replied, pulling on his robe. "Just a minute, if you please!"

He waited until I was safely secure behind the door of our adjoining rooms before he went to the door with a candle in hand. I listened on the other side of the door and then I heard Darcy address the person.

"Uncle Fitzwilliam?" Darcy said.

"Good evening, Darcy," I heard Earl Fitzwilliam reply. "Sorry, did I wake you?"

"No, you did not; I was just resting my eyes."

"Oh. I was wondering if I might be allowed to..."

"Oh, of course, come in. Come in."

I heard footsteps as Earl Fitzwilliam entered and I heard both men sit down.

"So, what do I owe the pleasure of my uncle coming to visit me at this hour?"

"I just wished to talk of what happened today."

"Oh, yes. That whole business. To be honest, I had quite forgotten about it already."

"Did you?"

"Uncle, I was being sarcastic."

"Oh, right. Of course, good man. Good man. Good man."

Earl Fitzwilliam continued to mumble like this for a bit, and a part of me felt quite sorry for him, because he was clearly disturbed about something.

"Uncle," Darcy said at last, "do you have something you wish to talk about, because forgive me, but this feels slightly awkward."

"Oh, of course. I was wondering. You are certain of this engagement of yours? You are fully committed to marrying Miss Elizabeth Bennet?"

"Of course, I am. I thought I was clear on that score."

"Yes, well, I just… are you really quite certain, Darcy?"

"I beg your pardon?"

"She is pretty, bright, charming, but well, as much as I hate to admit this, Catherine has a point. Is that enough for you in the end? If you marry Anne, you will have wealth, and both of you shall have Pemberly and Rosings Park between yourselves. Two of the greatest homes in England, and it shall belong to you both."

"And I care not for Rosings Park, nor do I care for Anne."

"I understand why not, for there is not much there to love, to be honest. Yet over time, sometimes the emotions fade. Sometimes people no longer love those who they were passionate about. I do not want to see you in love with a woman who one day you shall regret."

"Sir, I have been in love with women who I would go on to regret, and I know the experience. In truth, I have suffered greatly for it before. I was in love with another woman once, and she betrayed me. She quite betrayed me. Elizabeth Bennet is not that way. She makes me feel…I have always been my own man, but with her, I feel even more complete. She would never hurt me. It's not in her nature."

"Very well, it is just…I was just wishing to inquire, thinking about your future."

"There was a time where I did think of my future, Uncle, in regards to romance, and it resulted in being one of the worst decisions that I could have done. Well, I thank you, Uncle, but I must ask, why are you asking me this? Why do you speak to me? Rather, why do you not speak to your sons instead? Of course, you ought to let them alone, but I wonder why you consult your nephew and not your sons."

"Well, in truth, of course I have had my doubts, and I do secretly wish for them to marry women of wealth, but I know arguing with them is fruitless. For with one son, all of my wealth is settled irrevocably on and with the other, he inherits little, putting him out of my power quite so. All I could do was give them an example."

There was a slight pause in the conversation.

"Uncle, is there something else here?"

"Pardon?"

"You come to me. And you would not do that unless you had something to gain in it, I believe. I know that you care but, is the real reason that you come to me because you believe that if I leave Elizabeth, thus choosing Anne, then Zachary and Richard will follow my example, and they will abandon Lydia and Kitty, in order to find women of more sizable dowries. Am I right?"

There was another pause in the conversation.

"Uncle, am I correct?"

I heard the Earl sigh deeply. "Yes. I confess that I do wish that."

"Well, you cannot use me in that way, nor should you ought to. Uncle, if we did as our family desires, then that means we sent the Bennet sisters back to Longbourn, quite deceived and we have used them abominably ill. Is that really the sort of men that you want in your family? Is that the Fitzwilliam definition of chivalry? What sort of example would we set for our children and our families if we prove ourselves for being so cold?"

"I know. I feel like a monster for saying it, yet I had to inquire."

"Your inquiries would make mercenary monsters of us all. Is that what you wish?"

"No, of course not. It is just…these Bennet sisters bring no money with them. Richard will have to remain in the army, where he will have to risk his life. And Zachary might live beyond his means one day."

"I can assist them," Darcy said. "I have been making some investments, and their uncle is involved in trade. Perhaps when Richard is ready, he can find employment in the factory as a partner in some way. And I can help them both with investments. That, with the income they earn from Matlock's tenants, will be able to secure their future."

"I suppose you may be correct. Lady Fitzwilliam and I have had many a secret discussion on this matter. We both are happy and are not happy for them."

"End it and just be happy, because there is nothing you can do."

"This was not what I expected when you arrived here in Matlock with these sisters. Damn it all. What is it about those Bennet women that enraptures all? Well, besides their beauty of course."

"They are artless. They come to the relationships already aware of who they are. Believe me, that is rare."

"Yes, your aunt was like that with me. So self-aware, so dependable, so self-reliant."

"When you married my aunt, were you in love with her?"

"Well, it was a little different. She did have a bit of wealth to her dowry."

"Yes, but still, did you love her when you both met?"

"And she was very beautiful."

"And did you love her?"

"Well, yes. Yes, I admit that I did very much. She was also charming."

"And, if she were not wealthy, if she did not have the dowry, would that have impeded your love for her? And be truthful. Would it have?"

Once more, there was a bit of silence.

"No," Earl Fitzwilliam said at last. "No it would not have. I was so stubborn when I was young. I would have married her regardless."

"Precisely, so what made you believe that we would be any lesser in our ways?"

"I suppose not, for you are all Fitzwilliam men."

"Yes, we are. Uncle, none of us shall abandon them, because we ought not to."

"Right. Remember me when I am better, nephew. I just had to ask you all this because I ought to have."

"I understand."

"And mind you, I know that Elizabeth Bennet is your match."

"I am glad, for she is in every way."

"Then go to it, nephew. And the Bennet women shall be our family. I suppose, between Jane marrying your friend and the rest marrying us that only leaves Miss Mary to find her way."

"Yes, Miss Mary."

"Poor Miss Mary."

"Believe me, she is not poor. She is just going through a hard time. Hard times pass. I have had the experience to know it."

"But there is one thing."

"Yes?"

"Catherine, your aunt. She doesn't make empty threats. She is returning."

"You think so?"

"Oh, yes she is. Your Aunt Catherine will return, and you must be prepared for it."

"Well, I shall be."

Earl Fitzwilliam finally stood up, offered his goodnights and then left the room.

❧

I waited a full minute before I returned to Darcy's room.

"So," he began, "tell me, did you listen in on that entire conversation?"

"Yes, I did," I replied without shame.

"Yes, you did." He gave me a half smile.

"I always wondered why the Fitzwilliams accepted us Bennets as wives for their sons and you so easily, but now I see why. They never fully accepted it and were just waiting to phrase it in a way that would make it successful."

"Yes, it was too good to be true. So, all of them wanted my ancestor to marry this Anne de Bourgh?"

"It clearly is so."

"However, my ancestor proposed to you?"

"Yes, and he made no mention of this Anne de Bourgh at all when he did it. I promise you that this clearly means that there really is no real engagement between them."

"Yes, it clearly is the schemes of two women who got sentimental and fell into the joys of matchmaking, which mothers do either so very well, or so very terribly. In truth, when my mother met Caroline Bingley, my ex-wife, she hated her."

"She did?"

"Yes, and she thought that she wasn't good enough for me. I thought that was just her maternal instinct being too protective, but it turned out that she was actually accurate. She never trusted Caroline and said that she always had artfulness about her. And she was correct."

"Yes, she was. But I wonder if she would have liked me."

"She would have. And if not, who cares?"

I laughed and then rushed up to him. He raised me in his arms, we lay down on the bed and then we made love.

With my legs wrapped around his waist, Darcy entered me, and we became one once more, enjoying the comforts of the intimacy that we had reached in so natural a way always.

When complete, and having our fill, Darcy rolled over; I wrapped my arms around his back, holding him as he fell into a deep sleep.

Time had tested Mr. Darcy.

All of space and time had done it, and through it all, he proved to be the strongest man I had ever met. Strong enough for the past, for being out of time and out of place, thus making the desperate pleas of an earl who was still clinging to old ideals as if it was something that need never be heard or even considered.

Chapter Four

DOING ONES DUTY

Due to Zachary and Richard staunchly wishing to immerse Lydia and Kitty at Matlock, they had their parents invite us to remain at the estate for another fortnight before returning to Pemberly.

Darcy and I readily agreed to this, because it gave us all a chance to send out our letters to our parents, informing them that we would have a triple wedding, much to the happiness of our mother, and to the pleasant surprise of our father who wrote back with a simple reply:

Well now, in all my years, I never would have seen that coming

Therefore, we spent much time at Matlock, walking about the grounds, and Earl and Lady Matlock getting to know their future daughters-in-law once more. After fully accepting the idea and mingled with the prospect of a triple marriage to three sisters, Lady Fitzwilliam began to revel in the idea of helping us design and choose our wedding gowns.

"I refuse to have you married in your best Sunday gown, as is usual for weddings," Lady Fitzwilliam said, when she had a dresser come into her home and work on the designs. "No, I will not have that at all. And while I know that your parents of course wish for you both to get married in Hertfordshire, that will not do. This is a triple wedding, and it must be in a place where all the families here must see it. It will be the talk of the county and it will become a legend in Derbyshire."

"If there is anything that can rouse a mother from suspicion of a woman being good enough for her son," Darcy whispered to me throughout all this, "it is the wedding arrangements."

"Did the concept of wedding arrangements eventually bring your mother to like Caroline?" I asked him.

"Not even a little bit. And she even declared that if we married, Caroline would have the worst wedding gown imaginable."

"I wish she did!" I hissed. "But for the love of all that is holy, her wedding gown was lovely!"

"Yours will be lovely as well."

"Oh, but you must now know. In our time period, wedding gowns are rarely ever white."

"Really?"

"Yes, the idea of a white wedding gown does not come into effect until 1840, when Queen Victoria gets married."

"Is she born yet?"

"I do not think so. No, she is not, I am sure now. Yet when she will eventually get married, she will wear white to her wedding, and then it will become a trend. Who knows? Perhaps she gets the idea because one day we meet her, and we suggest it," I added playfully and in jest.

"What color would you prefer?"

"I think I have a better idea." I turned to Lady Fitzwilliam.

"Ah, madam," I asked her, "I am a little confused of what to wear for my wedding, in regards to the color of the gown. Can you offer some knowledge on what you think would be best for me?"

Lady Fitzwilliam was all aglow at this request.

"Oh, of course I should love to offer that, my dear. In fact, I propose that you all wear a set of colors that shall work well against your skin tones as well as suits your looks and complement one another."

"What suggestions?" Kitty asked, knocking her head playfully against Georgiana's as they giggled. "What color suits me?"

"Oh, with your skin tone, you would look beautiful in pink, Miss Kitty. And with you, Lydia, I think we should have a lovely light blue. Periwinkle would be the best color. And for you, Miss Elizabeth, to complement the glow of your skin and your dark hair against your dark eyes, I believe that light yellow shall be your perfect color."

"Pink, yellow, and blue," Mary said. "Yes, those colors shall suit very well."

"Oh, dear me!" Jane sighed. "I wonder now if I made a mistake and got married too early. Oh, never mind, for I very well believe that you all simply got married too late."

"I cannot argue with you there, Jane," Kitty said, "except that we had not met them yet."

"Or made them feel as if they had no choice but to fall in love with us either." With that, Lydia laughed, and we all joined in.

※

As we all planned away, I saw Georgiana smoothly disentangle herself from our company and sit herself next to Mary. Due to my placement, I was able to overhear them without appearing as if I was attempting to eavesdrop.

"I agree on their colors," Georgiana said, "you must be very happy for your sisters."

"I am, Miss Darcy," Mary said, "very much so."

"Really? Because I believe that this all does not interest you. Forgive me for being impertinent, but it is very well, Miss Mary, if planning weddings is not something that interests you."

"It is not so much that as it is… well, Miss Darcy, it is hard to say."

"Then that means that it must be spoken of. Usually the hardest things to speak of are the ones that are most important to speak about."

"Yes, well, it is only… for the longest time, I viewed all these things, from the idea of getting excited about a gown, to planning a wedding, as not something that could ignite my joy. In fact, or to put it more properly, I felt as if it ought not to excite me. After all, we are trained to find such materialistic views as being frivolous and counterproductive to our spiritual advancement. I viewed it as such, because it was right and correct to do so. And then I was engaged, and deep within, in truth, I began to find excitement at the idea of planning it all. I dared to admit to myself that there was something about me that was…"

"Just like the rest of us."

"Precisely. And then, when it was all taken away from me, I felt so very much embarrassed, but even when Jane married Mr. Bingley, I was not jealous. And yet, now it is very different. Now I feel a sad sort of envy. It is a sin, I know."

"Miss Mary, it is natural."

"I know that I ought to be happy for them, and I am. Yet I cannot rein my feelings in as I usually do."

"And again, it is natural, for jealousy is a natural emotion."

"It's a terrible vice."

"Because it's a popular one. In truth, I have been jealous before."

When Georgiana confessed this, Mary looked on her in wonder.

"What?"

"Yes."

"But it cannot be. You are wealthy and beautiful. Who could have made you jealous?"

"It was a couple of years ago, when I was in Ramsgate. While there, I noticed many a woman who was walking around with her beau, and they were madly in love—or they appeared to be to the mind of an idealistic girl who looked on them with longing and jealousy. In truth, age has given me a larger perspective and a more objective eye. And many of them only appeared to be in love while the woman was more about being seen with the man on her shoulder, wearing him like an ornament, and the men could often just be mercenary or superficial. Yet in my mind, they were all so beautiful, because they had a person beside them, and it gave them importance. It made them feel as if they mattered in the world."

"That is precisely what I felt when Mr. Collins and I were engaged," Mary confessed. "I felt as if I could be of use to someone in this world. I felt as if I mattered."

"Yes, I know the feeling." Georgiana heaved a sigh. "For that was the way I viewed Mr. Wickham."

"Was it?" Mary asked, tilting her head toward her.

"Yes. And now that I see it, I am prepared to admit that it was that jealousy of all those women I saw who appeared as happy that perhaps led to me falling in love with Mr. Wickham even quicker than I would have. Jealousy working on a vain mind creates many forms of mischief. I had seen a perfect image, and he was going to be the means through which I achieved my own version of it. And look what happened? Oh well, I've lived, and I have learned."

"I..."

"What?"

"Miss Darcy, take no offense to what I say, but I admit, when Lydia eloped, I hated her. And I viewed elopement as the worst of things. But you have done it?"

"Yes, I have," Georgiana answered, stoic.

"And yet you are different. With you, I see something else. It is simply, one does foolish things when one is in love."

"Precisely. Were you actually in love with Mr. Collins?"

"When I was to marry him, I felt as if I was doing my duty. And I love my duty. I suppose, now that I consider it, I had fallen more in love with the idea of doing my duty rather than being in love with him."

"Doing one's duty is always beneficial, especially since our only job, as women in our social sphere, is to get married. Yet while duty is important, what is your desire?"

"I have not considered it."

"Then do so. And see what you discover."

"What do you desire, Miss Darcy?"

"At the moment, I desire to stand on my own feet. It is a nice change."

I could not wait for Georgiana to finish talking so that I could thank her, when we were interrupted, where the steward entered.

"Master Fitzwilliam and mistress," he announced, "Lady Catherine's carriage has arrived."

Chapter Five

THE TICKING OF TIME

M y blood felt as if it ran cold, and all around me appeared as if it was frozen in time. No one moved, no one spoke and perhaps no one even breathed. Yet here was the moment that we all were braced for, without being fully braced for it.

Earl Fitzwilliam sighed, standing up. "Ah, well. I suppose I ought to go out and meet her, for there is no stopping this moment."

Earl Fitzwilliam took a few steps forward and yet he didn't have time to go out and meet his sister, for we heard the proud footsteps of the great lady even before we saw her.

"No, I shall not wait," Lady Catherine's voice boomed from the entranceway. Her footsteps grew louder as she appeared in the archway of the sitting room, filling the space with her pride.

However, she was not alone.

Behind her there was a woman. She was a young woman and was nicely dressed, to the point of being overdressed and gaudy looking, like a walking bit of upholstery, and her gown quite drowned her, for there was more of it than of her.

"Is that my cousin?" Darcy whispered to me, shocked.

"Yes, I do believe that it is," I answered, and the prospect was a bleak one that could not have made me happier. Anne de Bourgh looked sickly, clearly having the constitution of a hypochondriac, and she even looked a little cross and unpleasant. She looked as if she couldn't survive childbirth in a million years. And when she looked on Darcy, there was no smile, no hint of affection. There was only deadness, empty eyes and sullenness.

"Ah, my family who has quite turned my mind to sadness with all that I have given them," Lady Catherine said. "And how was I to be repaid? In ingratitude and coldness."

"That was not what you experienced," Darcy replied. "Hello Aunt Catherine."

"My nephew," she snorted. "The one who forgot his duty to his family, and his promise to me."

"I made no such promise."

"Really? Then tell that to your fiancée, for she is here."

Lady Catherine moved aside, and her daughter was now before us.

"So, that's my cousin," Darcy repeated to me.

"Yes, Miss Anne de Bourgh."

"You actually marry your cousins in this time. That is just repulsive!"

"Yes, I know that now."

Darcy turned to Anne, while I did not leave his side.

"Hello Fitzwilliam," Anne de Bourgh said.

"Good day, Anne," Darcy said, bowing to her.

"And good day, Miss de Bourgh," I said, curtsying to her. "My name is Miss Elizabeth Bennet."

"It is a pleasure to meet you," Anne said timidly, and then she curtsied to me eventually. It took her a moment to gather up the strength to do it, as she raised a handkerchief to her nose and blew into it.

"And I with you. Well, how was your journey? Were the roads dry?"

"Yes, they were."

And then the conversation shifted really quickly to awkwardness as Anne had nothing else to say.

"Well," I began, "do you have any questions for us? Forgive me, but I know not how to approach this situation. I know you must feel inconvenienced."

"She does at the very least!" Lady Catherine bellowed. "And at the very most she feels betrayed. For betrayal this is."

"Why not have her tell us, Lady Catherine?" I asked. "For surely, since she is involved in this, we ought to hear her say on the matter."

"She doesn't need to speak."

"Wait," Darcy interrupted. "I was supposed to marry her, and she doesn't even have a say in the matter?"

"I know what she intends, for I am her mother, and am aware of all her dearest concerns."

"Then as her mother, shouldn't your concern be to care about what she feels on matters? For at this point, all I know is that Anne had a pleasant trip here, but I know nothing about her feelings, her heart, or anything else. I don't even know if she wants to get married. All I know is that you want us to. But I am not marrying you, Aunt."

"Of course, you are not. What a strange notion!"

"It wasn't even a notion, so why do you talk like that!" I cried, at my wit's end. "So far, Lady Catherine, besides insulting me in every possible method, now you insult your daughter."

"I do nothing of the kind!"

"Yes, you do! You brought her all the way here, she looks as if she has been quite bullied into the matter, then you speak for her, showing that you do not even respect her enough to let her speak for herself."

"I respect my daughter; you may depend on it."

"Then let us hear her!" I demanded. "Let us hear what she thinks on the whole situation."

"She is very displeased."

"Then let us hear her say it, Aunt!" Darcy ordered. "Let me hear Anne tell me her sadness, so that I may explain myself."

"Miss de Bourgh," I explained, looking at Anne, "when I fell in love with your cousin, I had no idea of your existence, and Mr. Darcy meant no harm to you. In fact, he did not even view this idea of your engagement as a certain thing, but only a passing bit of folly that was exchanged without consulting either interested party at first. He was led to believe that there was not real agreement or understanding between you and he. He is not to blame, I can assure you, nor did he mean to hurt you. But if you tell us what you feel, we shall love to hear it."

Anne opened her mouth and then closed it.

"There, you see?" Lady Catherine bellowed. "She is so shocked at this all, so heartbroken, that she can't even speak it."

"I don't want to get married!" Anne cried.

When she spoke this, her mother flinched and turned to her.

"What did you say, Anne?"

"I said," Anne answered, lowering her voice to a whisper, looking thoroughly petrified, "that I do not want to get married. Fitzwilliam never loved me, and I never loved him."

"Upon my honor, what does love have to do with a fortunate alliance? Anne, you are not making any sense."

"Indeed, I am, and I do not want to marry him. Mama, I cannot do this any longer. What Aunt Darcy and you dreamed of was so many years ago. Please, do not make me go through with this!"

Lady Catherine threw up her hands and began to pace back and forth, irate.

"Indeed, the whole world is against me, and I deserve none of it! I, who have prided myself on my ability to always have my point carried out, as my right is to be so. I know all of your concerns and I will not be denied now, not so close to my hour of triumph."

"This is not your hour," Jane said, "this is their time."

"I did this for my daughter," Catherine shouted. "That is sacrifice. That is love!"

"It is not—" I began but I was quickly cut off as I began to hear a clock tick.

"Oh my god." I gasped, and then I turned to Darcy, who also looked shocked.

"You hear it?"

"Yes! You hear it too!"

"Yes," he said as I grabbed his hand.

"What on earth are you both talking about?" Lady Catherine bellowed.

"Oh, surely you can hear it?" Jane said.

Darcy and I turned to her.

"I had no idea that it was on the hour precisely," Jane continued.

"Jane, you can hear it too?" I voiced.

"Well, yes, of course I can. It's just a clock sounding off."

"What clock?" Bingley asked.

"Well, the clock, the time, is ticking away. It must be on the hour."

"There is no clock chime now," Earl Fitzwilliam said, "for it is only 1:20 in the afternoon. You are making no sense."

"No, she is making perfect sense," Kitty said. "For it is going off."

We both turned to Kitty and blinked.

"Kitty, you hear it too?"

"Yes! Of course, I do. And why am I all wet?"

"I hear nothing," Lydia said.

"But my dear, of course you must hear it," Zachary Fitzwilliam said, "for it is loud and clear."

"You hear it too?" Darcy asked.

"Yes, of course I do. Lydia, my love, you joke now. Surely you hear it."

"Yes," Mary said, "for it is as loud as day. Oh, it is getting louder now."

"Indeed, it is," Georgiana also added, to our surprise. "Dear me, it is hurting my ears. And my clothing is all wet!"

"What are you all on about?" Colonel Fitzwilliam cried, and then he turned to Kitty, who now appeared as if she had just stepped out of a lake.

"Richard," Kitty cried, "what is happening to me?"

Colonel Fitzwilliam looked flabbergasted.

"Kitty, you're drenched!"

"Oh no, not them!" I was terrified, seeing what was about to occur. "Colonel and Zachary, grab ahold of Kitty and Lydia. Do it now!"

"What the devil are you on about?" Lady Catherine cried. "And what are you playing at?"

She continued to drone on and on, but her voice was drowned out by all the sounds of a clock, the ticking of time, and the next thing we all knew, we were being pulled under, far away, and through time and space.

My eyes closed as all went black, where I knew that there was no point in struggling.

And yet, this time it was different. From what I recalled, I always remembered the clock being the most incredible and overpowering thing when this occurred. Yet this time, it was a blue light as I felt that I was swiveling around in over and over.

"Darcy!" I cried.

"I'm here, Elizabeth," I heard him reply, and then I felt someone grab my hand, and I knew it was him. Yet the light was too powerful, too blinding, but I knew that we were being jerked forward, or backwards, or to the right or to the left.

The sound of the clock grew louder and louder, and then it stopped just as I knew it would, and I felt my body lying on something hard, with Darcy's hand still in mine.

"I was not in water this time." I gave a shaky sigh, rubbing the part of my body that was bruised from landing. "I don't understand. It used to be water that carried us."

"Not always though." Darcy lay nearby, then he lowered his body over mine. "Elizabeth, are you hurt?"

"I am well enough," I said. "Are you well?"

"Just a little bruised, but no matter."

"Yes, and…" Now that my mind was adjusted, I realized that we surely would not have been alone. "But wait! What of Kitty, Georgiana, and Mary?"

"Elizabeth!" Kitty cried. "Is that you?"

Darcy and I sat up, rolled over and just a short distance away, we saw Kitty as she was helping up a man. Then we saw Mary as she was assisting Georgiana and Jane also was getting to her knees.

They had followed us! Why the devil were they forced to do that?

Darcy and I stood up and looked around and saw the curious looks of many people on the street, the familiar street where Darcy once lived. They looked on us as if they were spooked creatures, not understanding what we were about, and their clothing, their 21st century clothing said it all. From the trousers on women to the headphones that were in people's ears as they gave us blank stares.

"Darcy, are we back in Mayfair?" I asked.

"Bloody hell!" he gasped. "I'm home!"

He looked up to his left, and there was the familiar door to his home that we had entered so very often.

"I'm at my home and do not have a key to it," he said. "How bloody strange it all is."

❦

We were in fact returned back in the future, or Darcy's present, or judging by the day, even perhaps his past.

With alacrity, we rushed to our family and were surprised to see that the man Kitty was helping up was indeed Zachary Fitzwilliam. Of course, he had heard the clock, but why him? At least Georgiana, Jane, Kitty, and Mary made some strange sense, because they were at least more connected to us, but Zachary was a strange victim of the circumstance.

As they all stood, I felt an immense pity for them. There they were, wet through and through, standing on a street in London in the future, and they would be entirely lost, and it was even more tragic for two reasons.

"What happened?" Zachary Fitzwilliam gasped, looking around, utterly distraught. "Where are we? And where is Lydia?"

"And where is Richard!" Kitty cried.

"And Charles!" Jane stressed. "Where is Charles?"

She then ran about, looking around things and avoiding people's looks of horror at seeing her, and then turned back to us.

"Where is my husband? Dear god, what happened to us, and where is he?"

We had fallen forward into the future and it was clear that Lydia, Mr. Bingley, and Colonel Fitzwilliam were left behind. Back in Darcy's past and in my present.

"Jane, Kitty, Lydia, Mary, and Mr. Fitzwilliam," I murmured, "I am sorry. I am so, so, so very sorry, but they are not here."

"What do you mean they are not here?" Kitty cried. "And where are we anyway? And they must be here."

"And again, where are we?" Mary stressed.

"You are in London," Mr. Darcy said.

"What!" Zachary shouted. "But we were just in Derbyshire. We were always in Derbyshire."

"You're in London now, Mayfair to be exact."

"But this is not London," Georgiana refuted, looking around at passersby. "Look at everyone."

"Precisely," Mary magnified. "People do not dress like this in London, or anywhere."

"Not anywhere in your time," Darcy confessed, "because you're in the future. And my present."

"What?" Georgiana questioned. "Brother, what are you talking about?"

"I'm talking about the fact that you're not in 1812, but rather you are in the year 2016."

"What?"

"Look around. And you all heard the clocks yourself. You have been transported through time and are now in the future. Like Elizabeth said, you are in London, in the 21st century. In 2016."

"But that's impossible," Zachary declared.

"But it happened," I said. "Darcy is correct, and I can assure you this is all real. You are not dreaming. Look at it all yourself. You're in the future, for this is not London as you know it, but it's London all the same."

"Even if that is possible, which it isn't," Georgiana inferred, "Fitz, why do you know about that?"

Darcy looked to me, but he did not have time to respond, because the door to his home opened and a woman quickly emerged out of it.

"Fitzwilliam!" she exclaimed. "My goodness, don't worry! You were only gone for a few minutes in our time. How long were you pushed into the past?"

My breath was caught in my throat as I beheld her. At first, she was all attentive to Darcy, rushing up to him and imploringly looking at him only. Yet when he looked down on her with quiet alarm, she at last looked on the rest of us and her eyes fell on me.

"Oh my god!" she gasped.

"Dear lord," I exclaimed, yet there could have been no real words that would accurately describe what I was feeling, or what she must have been. At first, I didn't believe it. Or I did not wish to believe it. Such a thing was impossible.

And yet I knew that it was very much possible, and that it did happen. It had always happened, and now it was just time to face it.

There, before me, stood the woman who fell back in time when I fell forward and took her place.

The Elizabeth of the past, I was.

The Elizabeth of the future, she was.

We both, not one difference in feature, but literally looking exactly alike, were staring back at each other.

Chapter Six

TWO ELIZABETHS

"I ..." I began, but words failed me even more than they failed her apparently, for very soon she looked thunderstruck and as if she wished me to be on the other side of the world.

She covered her mouth with her hand, which was shaking. "My god, we really do look exactly alike?"

"You know about me? How do you?"

"Because of him," she said, pointing to Darcy, who looked absolutely shocked as he looked between us.

"What do you mean?" I asked.

"How did you get here?"

"The same way that you got to my time so long ago. Because of time."

"I only fell through time twice. It seems as if you did it more. And all these years, I thought it was from something that you did. I thought I fell through time because of you!"

I answered, "If it is such, it's not my fault. And what did you mean by all those years? How long has it been since you switched places with me?"

This Elizabeth did not answer me as she looked me up and down.

"You?" she began. "You cannot be here."

"But I am," I answered.

"But you shouldn't be. This is my time and I will not let you have him again."

When she said this, she gestured to Darcy.

36

"What do you mean by that?" Darcy asked. "Forgive me, but I am truly confused now."

"How are you, Fitz?" she asked, looking between us both and then she took his hand, looking alarmed. "You could not have forgotten me."

"Forgive me," he said, looking between us both again, "but I cannot tell you at all what the bloody hell is going on."

Elizabeth looked between us both and then at me, her look filled with venom.

"What did you do to him?"

"I did nothing. And why are you so angry at seeing me?"

"Because I know how he felt for... did he lose his memory when he fell through time? Is that why he cannot remember me?"

"I'm sorry!" Zachary Fitzwilliam roared. "But what in the name of Saint Peter are you getting on about?"

This other Elizabeth was pulled out of her pity-party and she turned to the rest of the group, then she looked on my sisters.

"Kitty, Mary... and Jane!"

"But," Mary gasped, "what is happening here? And who are you? And how do you both look identical?"

"Because we are related in two different time periods," the other Elizabeth said, and then she turned to me. "Because I am her great-great-great-great-great grandniece." Of this, I felt entirely at a loss. My head spun and my heart nearly broke my ribs. That was how shocked I was.

"What? What?"

"When I fell back into the future," she continued, "I did research. I'm your distant descendant, and I keep being manipulated by time all because of you or something else that is really rubbish. At first it was annoying, but this was frightening. After all," she added, turning back to Darcy, "as you can imagine, now the time is different. And surely you must be able to remember this all somehow. Even a little bit. I cannot have time separate us just now, so when you disappeared an hour ago when we were in the living room, I was so scared. I almost fainted."

"What do you mean that I disappeared an hour ago?" Darcy asked.

"Oh," Elizabeth said, turning to me, "now time has broken his mind. What happened to him?"

"Wait," I said. "If I am to understand this right, you think this is...do you think this is his ancestor?"

When I asked her this, Elizabeth's face became quite flushed.

"Well, of course it is, of course it is… this is Mr. Fitzwilliam Darcy, and we are married."

I bit my lip and looked up at Darcy, who looked as if he could have been knocked down with a feather.

"We are not married," he replied simply. "I would have known I had gotten married if I had."

"No, you aren't married to him," I finished. "And you are now beginning to realize it. You thought he was your Mr. Darcy, which means that he had fallen through time right here, and you eventually became married, and now he has fallen back in time, and we have fallen forward."

"No," Elizabeth said, although there was doubt in her voice.

"Yes. I'm sorry, Miss Elizabeth, but this is Mr. Darcy, my fiancé, and your Mr. Darcy has fallen back into 1812 again."

Elizabeth was flabbergasted, but while I was as well, I had to quiet my alarm, because it was not going to be helpful. This woman was my descendant! That's why she fell in time in my place, and I fell into hers. We were linked in a strange way for some reason, and therefore our lifelines were reliant on the other in a perverse sort of way. And Mr. Darcy had found his way to this time, and clearly he had been there for a while.

"Miss Elizabeth," I continued, trying to be calm, "what year is it? It's not 2016, is it?"

"No," she whispered, "it's 2022. And Mr. Darcy and I have been married for five years."

"Five years?" I marveled. "He was here for all that time and then married to you?"

"Yes, he was," she affirmed, her air somber as the reality began to move from the state of being in denial to the state of painful acceptance. She looked back at Darcy and then at me once more. "He's not my husband?"

"No, I am so very sorry. He's not."

"And again, what is all this damned nonsense about?" Zachary railed.

I leaned forward and looked at Elizabeth once more.

"Miss Elizabeth," I said, "please. I know what you must be experiencing right now."

"Where is my Mr. Darcy?"

"Miss Elizabeth!"

"Where is my Mr. Darcy?"

I bit my lip and then had no choice but to admit the reality again.

"He would probably have returned to the past. He would still be in 1812 right now."

Elizabeth covered her mouth and was about to begin weeping, but I knew that we could no longer stand there.

"Miss Elizabeth, you are my descendant, so clearly you know that you owe me something."

"I owe you something?"

"Yes, you owe me your existence somehow, for all that you know. Therefore, you shall have to do me this favor. Please, we can speak on this later, but until then, please invite us in, for we have nowhere to go right now."

Elizabeth rubbed her lip with her hand and then she considered this very quickly.

"Right," she said. "Come in."

We all followed her inside, where all of us were in a strange state, but it was my sisters, Georgiana and Zachary who were in the worst state of all, for they still had no idea what was fully going on.

৩৯৩

As we entered, with the exception of Darcy and me, all of them looked around in wonder at Miss Elizabeth's home, while I mostly just stared at her as she led us in.

"What sort of house is this?" Georgiana asked under her breath.

"It's the 21st century kind," Elizabeth said coldly. "You'll get used to it quickly, for he did."

At that point, I knew that Elizabeth was upset, but there was nothing to be done.

"This is my home!" Darcy blurted out, as he walked around the living room. "My god, it's changed so much since then."

"Well, it's his home now," Elizabeth said, still secretly fuming. It was very clear that the very sight of us antagonized her.

"What do you mean that this is your home?" Georgiana inquired, perplexed. "And what is all of this about?"

"Are you thirsty?" Elizabeth asked, "or hungry? Despite it all, don't say that I have lost my manners."

"We are fine at the moment," Darcy said. "It's just important that we get things cleared up. But thank you."

"Forgive me, but who are all these people?" Elizabeth asked, pointing to the rest of our group. "The way I understand it, falling into time was something only we were victims to."

"Yes, well, we did not see this coming." Darcy then turned sadly to Georgiana. "And this is his little sister."

"Oh." Elizabeth shifted in her seat, then stood up and her whole demeanor changed, as it would have. For this would have been her sister-in-law. "Hello, Miss Darcy, I have heard so much about you, and I am...I know you must be confused, but I am delighted to make your acquaintance."

"But... I do not understand." She then turned to Darcy, who looked down at his feet.

"Sorry, Georgiana, and you all," I said, "for we are not explaining this properly."

"You fell through time," Elizabeth said. "You fell through a wormhole if you will."

"A wormhole?" Zachary echoed.

"That was all that I could discover when I fell back into my own time," she explained, "when I fell back into 2016. I read up on all the latest theories of time travel. According to all, it of course is still deemed impossible, but it is as if it is another dimension entirely. If there is a way to travel through time, which we now know that it is such, we must have fallen through a wormhole, a chink in time, or another dimension entirely within the layers of the universe. Of course, we never discovered how."

"Forgive me," Zachary bellowed, "but nothing you say makes any sort of sense."

"We must consider them," I said to Elizabeth, who it would always be so strange to look on. "For we are speaking in a way that would alarm them. Georgiana, Kitty, Mary, Jane and Zachary, you have all just time travelled."

"Time travelled?" Mary echoed.

"Yes, you fell from our time, were transmitted through the years and now we have been placed in 2022, over two hundred years into the future."

"Impossible. Time travel could never occur."

"It has, and I can prove it. Besides, you've seen it for yourselves. You experienced it for yourself."

"You can prove it?"

"Well, besides that we are in it now—"

"That means nothing," Zachary interrupted. "Because we are just in the midst of a dirty trick. Some sort of sordid joke that is being played on us."

"I know you wish to believe so, but it is not the case at all," I continued. "I can prove that we have fallen through time, because this is not the first time that I have. Mary, Kitty and Jane, do you remember, all those months ago, when I came home wearing strange clothing and I was soaking wet?"

"Yes," Jane said, "and I had thought that…" Jane trailed off and she had looked at my descendant.

"You were so kind to me when I appeared at Longbourn," Elizabeth added softly, "and I thank you for that, truly, for I know that I must have appeared as being quite bewildering."

Jane and Kitty looked at me in wonder.

"But," Jane continued, looking at me, "you said that you were confused. When I expressed my worries, my belief that there was something else occurring, something foul, you refuted it."

"But Jane, what was I to say?" I countered. "If I had told you that she and I did change places, that the woman you cared for was indeed not myself, but a person from the future while I took her place here, would you not have thought me mad?"

"Oh, I see. I would not have regarded it as being true."

"No, I could not blame you for it as well. What happened was that I was transported to the future, this Elizabeth took my place in Longbourn, and I was here, in the 21st century, for months, almost a year."

"You were in this time period for almost a year?" Kitty said, stunned. "Almost a whole year?"

"Yes."

"You were by yourself? I'm not in the mood to deny what is before me, because it is pointless, therefore I shall roar out in fear later on, because now there are more pressing matters than for me to give in to hysterics," And here Elizabeth chuckled, half-bitterly and half-amused, "but Elizabeth, dear god, how did you survive the future all on your own?"

"I didn't," I said, looking at Darcy, and Georgiana followed my eyes. "What I mean is that I was not alone."

"What did you mean," Georgiana asked, "when you called me 'his sister'?" she asked Darcy, who bit his lip, his eyes turned to me and he did not know what to say.

"He meant just that," Elizabeth answered for us both. "Sorry to tell you this, Miss Darcy, and I know that you will despise this all, but this is no one's fault. I can see that you let her believe that you were her brother, huh?" Elizabeth asked Darcy.

"I had no choice."

"I know, I know. And I'm not upset; I just wished to be clear." Elizabeth's look was sad as she looked at Darcy wistfully. "You look so much like him. And that's what's hardest. This hurts, this hurts so much."

"I know the feeling," I said to her. "I know how it feels to be separated from my own love for even longer than you hopefully shall not have to endure."

"And we... we look..."

"Yes, we do. Precisely alike."

"To the point that it is weird."

"Bloody weird."

"Yes, absolutely bonkers." Elizabeth turned back to Georgiana. "He never meant to deceive you, please believe it. No one did. But that man there, he is not your brother."

Georgiana blinked, very confused. "Of course he is."

"No, I am not," Darcy said at last, looking repentant. "Georgiana, I am sorry, but I am not."

"You're speaking nonsense, all of you," Georgiana refuted, overcome with denial.

"Georgiana," I asserted, feeling most sorry for her, for she deserved so much better, "we never meant to hurt you, but we just did not want you to undergo such pain."

Her eyes grew cold, she took a step back, her expression turned to stone, and I knew what I was beholding; it was of a woman who did not want to accept all that was before her, but she was doing so nonetheless. She was preparing herself for something she neither wanted to hear nor accept.

"If what you say is true then... where is my brother?"

"We cannot know for sure, but if I am correct," I explained, "he would have returned to your time, to the 19th century."

"If he returned when we fell through here, then that means he was here to begin with."

"Yes, it does," I answered shakily.

"How could that be?"

"We don't know why this is happening."

"When was the last time that I saw my brother?" she questioned, not looking at us as she spoke it. "When did I really see him?"

I looked at Darcy and he flinched.

"When I came to the house wet all over and wearing those clothes that were strange to you all," he explained. "That was the day that we switched places."

"That was why you always were so curious about me," she whispered. "You were not gaining interest, but you simply were trying to trick me into thinking you were him."

"Georgiana, he had no choice," I defended. "He truly did not have a choice at all. He did everything in his power to stand in the place of a man he never met and make you happy."

"I know but I cannot…" She looked so terrified, but also at a loss. "I cannot… I know not what to do now."

"It is fine, take your time."

Georgiana turned back to us at last. "You took his place. All this time I thought I was speaking with my brother, walking alongside him and it was all a lie."

He sighed and ran his fingers through his hair. "Georgiana, please…"

"I know I should not hate you, for I can see why you did what you did, and I also can see how kind you have been, but I feel, I feel as if I am so terribly betrayed now."

"I never meant to betray you."

"Yes, I know, but now, all that I thought was a lie and I cannot, in all my power, remain composed. I cannot look on any of you now."

She rushed out of the room and yet I did not know where she would go, for it wasn't her home, but Mary stood up.

"I shall go to her," she said. "She just needs a moment."

"I should help," Elizabeth said.

"No, don't," I told her. "For the sight of you or me would only antagonize her."

"The way we antagonize each other with our presence." Elizabeth chuckled sadly as Mary tended to Georgiana. "Is that what we both know?"

"We have both been imposed upon," I told her.

"With you it is not so very hard," she countered, "for you still have your Mr. Darcy. Mine is driven from me for some cold reason."

"I suffered as well, and you know it."

"Do I?" Elizabeth smiled sadly. "Yes, I suppose you have."

"I very much have," I said, turning to Darcy. "I fell into the future, woke up in a river for some reason, and now we don't even have to be in water for this all to occur. And then when I finally won him, I got snatched away, back home, and was left there for months, thinking I was separated from him forever. Believe me, madam, if I was not doing everything in my power to remain calm, I would have shown you the pains I suffered with a lamentation. And it would have been proof enough for my sadness, even putting your current one to shame."

When she heard this, Elizabeth quieted and sat down. Her eyes grew moist. Though tears did not come, she was at the beginning of weeping, it was clear.

She lowered her head. "He left me, then. We worried about this for years. He left me and he might never come back."

"I'm sorry," I whispered, "yet he will come back."

"I should have been near him for longer," she said, "but we both grew so careless, and believed that we were no longer in danger. And yet it appears that we were in error on that. For we very much now were not so. He could have been pulled away from me at any moment."

"You should not blame yourself," Darcy said at last.

Elizabeth gave him a hard look. "Forgive me. It is only that seeing your face hurts me. It's not fair, you see, to see you and know that I might never see him again. What tedious rubbish!"

Mr. Darcy chuckled.

"Right, sorry," Elizabeth said, wiping her eyes. "I have not offered you that tea that I said I was going to. And you might even be hungry. This is England, and let it not be said that I lost my manners fully. Besides, it wasn't just two that came into time this way, for you have more with you," she said, looking at Kitty, Jane and Zachary. "Why the bloody hell would Time have toyed with you lot as well?"

Kitty looked at Jane, who was still slightly stunned, and Zachary was just too enraged at this all, so she opened her mouth.

"We do not fully know, and therefore—"

She was interrupted when the front door of their home opened, and then Elizabeth froze.

"Mum and Dad!" came the voice of a little girl, "Fred and I are back!"

"Yes, ma'am," came the voice of someone who clearly was watching them, "we are home."

⊛

Elizabeth sprang up like a jack in the box as we all froze. Her children had come home, and nothing would shock them more than seeing two of her, and their father dressed in strange clothes.

"You must go upstairs, and hide in the bedroom," she rushed out, ordering us all. "Go that way and use the back steps. The guest room is the third on the right and close the door behind you."

"But where are Mary and Georgiana now?" Jane pointed out.

"Don't worry about them," Elizabeth said. "I'll think of something. But my children cannot see you! So please, go!"

Darcy took my hand, gestured for all of us to follow him and we then began to race up the back steps.

"I just realized," I said as I was so close to him, "you are back in your old home."

"Yes, I am."

"How does it feel?"

"Like happiness."

We went upstairs to the guest room and closed the door behind us.

"I hope Georgiana does not hate me," he said.

"I'm sure that she doesn't," I comforted. "She just suffered a shock."

"A shock that she could easily blame me for."

"Don't worry, I shall talk with her."

"Well, talk with us first!" Zachary Fitzwilliam demanded. "And tell us that we had best be dreaming now."

"No, Mr. Fitzwilliam," Kitty answered for me, "we are not. I want to believe that we are but denying things shall seem to be useless at this point." Kitty then turned back to me. "We really fell through time?"

"Yes, we all did."

"Then that means…that I am separated from the Colonel?"

"And I am separated from Mr. Bingley," Jane whispered.

"And Lydia!" Zachary bellowed and then he lowered his voice, "Lydia is not here. She will not follow me."

"She might," I reassured him, "there is always a chance."

We were distracted when the door opened and Mary entered, followed by Georgiana. When she took a look at both of us, she opened her mouth, but then clearly did not trust herself to speak to Darcy or me; therefore she moved to the other side of the room and looked out of the window.

In truth, I wondered if there was a proper way to speak in her circumstance, a right way to behave or to act, but there was none. Nothing could prepare either of us for what we wished to say; therefore there was no right or wrong way to approach the situation.

"I think I speak for Georgiana," Mary said, "when I tell you that you need to tell us all this from the beginning."

"Yes, that would be wisest," Zachary said, taking a seat. "Perhaps if we think hard on this matter, we can discover a way to return, for I cannot bear this dreadful place."

"There is no way to return."

"You do not know that for sure," he snapped.

"But I do. I am sorry for it, sir."

"Well," he replied proudly, "I have to hope anyway, and I will. I did not find Lydia only to lose her to this nonsense."

I smiled at his stubbornness and looked at Georgiana.

"Please do not hate Darcy."

"He is not a Darcy," Georgiana retorted.

"I am though," Darcy replied. "I still am a Darcy. I am just simply not your brother."

"Fine then, who are you in full?"

"Georgiana," I said, "please understand, we just wished to not break your heart."

"And here I was, thinking I was on equal footing with you all, and I was not. It is just, it has set me down, you must understand. It very much has set me down." She was on the verge of tears.

"We can understand."

"Well, pray continue," Georgiana said, "mercy, I pray that we leave this place soon, and pray tell, how is it that there are two Mr. Darcys, and clearly two Elizabeths?"

Chapter Seven

THE EXPLANATION

" ... And that is how we ended up here," I concluded as I finished telling them my narration. They had been told everything, from when I had first fallen, to waking up in America, then to falling back into the past and now to us being brought there. As I finished, Kitty, Jane, Mary, Zachary and Georgiana looked at each other.

"Then it was true," Jane voiced at last. "All those months ago, when that other Elizabeth came to Longbourn and I had suspected..."

"Yes," I confirmed, "yes, you were correct. It was in fact not me. It was her all along."

"But when I had my suspicions, you denied them. Lizzy, why did you not tell me?"

"Again, I couldn't. Jane, like I said before, if I had, would you have believed me? I could not risk being thought insane."

"I know, but...well, I wish you would have trusted me, for I know very well that you are not insane at all. I thought perhaps I had temporarily gone mad myself for being paranoid."

"You did?"

"Yes, I did, for I truly believed that two different women had come to Longbourn that day and that you simply just looked alike, and now I know that I was not mentality imbalanced."

I touched her arm. "No, you were not. Oh, Jane I feel awful about it, really."

"So, I was not the only one who was deceived?" Georgiana whispered sadly. "Well then…"

"Oh, for god sakes," Kitty said sharply, "can we all stop acting as if this is their fault? It's not, and while I wish to believe that this is all not real, it clearly is, and complaining about it won't change anything."

"Kitty is correct," Mary said. "Mr. Darcy and Lizzy are just as much victims of this circumstance as the rest of us. We are all just upset for we are…"

"Thrown into a world that you are a stranger to and have no answers," Darcy finished for her. "Yes, I felt the same way that you feel now when I first fell back into your time. I promise you, the only one of us who was even fully inconvenienced, to my knowledge, was Lizzy here." He turned toward me and smiled.

"When she first fell into her future, she had none of you as a companion, and we met each other through accident where I hit her with my car."

"And what precisely is a car again?" Mary asked.

"Oh, you saw them parked along the street outside. They're like moving carriages that run on gas and you don't need horses."

Mary shuddered. "Sounds frightening."

"They can be death traps sometimes."

They all looked at us, horrified.

"Oh, sorry, perhaps I should not have said that."

"So," Zachary began, turning to Darcy, "you're not my cousin? He really has been trapped here, while you had to pretend to be him."

"If I had not," Darcy said, "and told you all the truth, you would have locked me away, thinking I am mad. Don't even deny it."

"I won't, for I know that Lady Catherine would have done just that."

Darcy shook his head and groaned. "After meeting her, I am certain that she would have."

"I will not blame you for any of this, I just…how long did you have to wait to see each other again?"

Darcy and I looked at each other.

"Well, it depended," Jane said. "For Elizabeth and the other Elizabeth both appeared at Longbourn on the same day, but then you say you were here for months."

I nodded. "Yes, I was. Time can work differently, but it seems that whenever I was in this era, I was here for months while it was merely a matter of hours in the past. Then when I fell into the past, it was months when it was merely hours for Darcy in the present until he came to the past and found me."

"Then, I could be here for months, but for Lydia, it could be a matter of minutes for her. Or it would be worse, where I could be here for minutes, while it is months for her."

"Or even years," Kitty said on a sigh. "The Colonel would think I abandoned him perhaps. And I had to fight to get him!" She seemed to blink back tears.

"And Mr. Bingley." Jane began to weep. "He would think he lost me! I cannot lose him, for what if he chooses another woman?"

"He would not do that," Georgiana said, "nor would the Colonel."

"But what about Lydia?" Zachary replied, looking very insecure. "Would she wait for me? She's a lively and charming woman and what if another man…"

"She will not want another man," Kitty confirmed. "She knows that she grew quite lucky when she found you. And she loves you, for she has told me so over and over to the point where I wished for her to be quiet."

Zachery appeared to relax. "Oh, that is comforting. Are you certain though?"

"Yes," we all said in unison, to which Zachary Fitzwilliam bit his lip, attempting to hide his sense of self-satisfaction. Yet I thought on what I had told him, and I was able to make a connection that I had not done so before.

"You do not need to worry about losing Lydia, Bingley or the Colonel," I assured them. "For the way that this works, time only moves slowly for the one who travels through it. For Darcy, when you fell through time and arrived at Pemberly, it had been a matter of hours. And at Longbourn when I left you, it was only hours for you. I was the one who moved through time, and it moved slowly for me, but not for those who remained left behind. And then the other Mr. Darcy—"

"Now you mean my brother," Georgiana clarified.

"Aye, him. He fell through time, and what was a couple months for us, it was five years for him. Therefore, when we do return, it should not be long for them."

"But it can be years for us," Mary confirmed.

"Yet therein is the problem now," Kitty focused. "Yes, we moved through time, but so did the other Mr. Darcy. Since both moved through time, can it be long for both of us all at once?"

"Oh, I had not thought of that," I answered.

"Yes, I see. Oh dear, I am making it more complicated."

"No, you are not and thank you, Kitty. It's just a complicated situation all around."

"Fitz," Georgiana announced suddenly.

Her expression was still as if she had turned to stone and Darcy froze when looking at her.

"Georgiana…"

"Don't worry, I'm not going to reprimand, berate, or place blame any longer. It is just… I thought we had come so far as brother and sister over these months, and to find out that it was not real."

"But it was though," Zachary spoke up, to our surprise. "He may not be your real brother or my cousin, but Georgiana, everything else that happened is real. Besides, I noticed the growth you had undergone since his arrival, and I am not sure that it all would have come about if it were not for this sudden exchange of persons."

"Thank you, Zach," Darcy assented, truly grateful.

I smiled at Zachery. "Well, you are truly full of surprises."

"I try, thank you."

"And that's why Lydia must actually love you so much."

"Yes, well, keep telling me that from time to time."

We were interrupted when the door opened and Elizabeth entered, carrying many modern day clothes.

"I got these for you, because it's very obvious that you will get beat up if you walk around like that outside."

Chapter Eight

SAD STORIES

"**W**here are your children?" I asked her.

"They are in their room with their nanny," she answered, handing the clothes to us individually. "This all should fit you because you ladies are all luckily around my build and these are my husband's clothes, which I know that you shall fit easily."

"But what room should we go to change in?" Mary asked.

"You all must change in here."

Mary, Jane, Kitty and Georgiana looked flabbergasted.

"But there are men in the room," Jane whispered. "Dear me, Miss Elizabeth, we cannot possibly…"

"We have to," I interrupted, not wanting to annoy my descendant any more than my appearance there had already done so. "The gentlemen will just have to turn around while we change. And don't worry; I shall help you put the clothes on correctly."

"I'm sorry for how I was earlier," Elizabeth said, calmer than she was before. "How are you all? Are you taking to this all better? I know it must be quite a shock."

"Thank you," Mary said, "yes, we have learned everything since then, and while we still are in denial slightly, we are beginning to adjust. And thank you for accommodating us."

"Well, you all did the same for me."

"You really were the one that I helped all those months ago," Jane voiced, "when you kept saying that you were not my sister."

"Yes, and you were all kind to me. I really must have unnerved you all."

"We understand now, and it is nice to make your acquaintance."

"Pleased to meet you as well, officially."

I looked at Elizabeth closely as she handed me a pair of jeans.

"How are you really?" I whispered to her. "You appear to be somewhat better."

"I'm fine, I'm just…"

"No, you are not fine. I can tell that you are still disturbed."

"Yes, I am a bit. Yet I see now that constantly complaining and blaming you all won't help at all."

"What about your children?"

"That is what I need to talk to you about. When you have made sure that the girls here have gotten dressed, I'll be in my husband's study. Come there as soon as you can. But don't bring him with you," she said, gesturing to Darcy.

"But I cannot, or don't want to," I refuted. "For I do not like being too far away from him for long."

"I can understand that, but I…the sight of him antagonizes me and I don't want to ever look at him."

I could understand that. "Right."

She smiled to us all and left.

"Well, at least she is looking better," Darcy said.

"Yes, yes she is."

When I made sure that the women were dressed in full, I went to leave the room, but Darcy was upset about letting me walk alone. I assured him that if I felt any sign of getting wet from time, then I would rush to him. Eager to satisfy the wife of his descendant, he then let me go, and eventually I crept out of the room, hoping no children would see me. I knocked on the study door and Elizabeth told me to come in. I did so, then closed the door completely behind me and turned to her.

There she was, the spitting image of me, staring back at me with a calmness that held tension underneath, and she was sitting at the desk.

"This was his study."

"Mr. Darcy's?"

"Yes. Or at least, *my* Mr. Darcy."

"Yes, your Mr. Darcy. But also mine. For you must recall that before you met him, his descendant owned this house and therefore, it is also his."

Elizabeth's face covered with worry. "What does that mean?"

"It means that we need your help."

"You made it seem like you were going to try and take over the home and take it from me."

I was taken aback. "Do you really think that I would do that?"

"I don't know. I just met you. We just look exactly alike, but we are not the same. Just as they look exactly alike and are not the same either."

"Do you think me some sort of cancer?" I asked her, worried about how this was going. I knew that she logically should not be too overjoyed about the situation, but now that we were in the midst of it, I hoped she would have been better about it.

She glanced at her hands, which were folded on top of the desk. "No, I don't. I'm just heartbroken."

"Well, when I thought I would never see my Mr. Darcy again, I felt the same thing, but I had to make do."

"He left me behind, with two children," she replied, "and yours got left behind, where, from what I understand, you had his ancestor who fell in love with you."

In hearing her speak, I drummed my fingers against the jeans on my thighs, now seeing why she was so apprehensive. Could it be? Was she jealous?

The house was familiar enough to me, so I just simply pulled up a chair and sat down on the other side of the desk.

"Elizabeth, what do you know about my past with your husband?"

Elizabeth looked down again.

"Everything, I believe. I know about how you met him at an assembly dance in Meryton, how you became further acquainted with him at his friend's estate at Netherfield Park. How you saved his life, which I am grateful for, truly I am. And then he became very attached to you there. He even invited you to Pemberly, where you met his cousin."

"Colonel Fitzwilliam."

"Yes. And he fell in love with you as well, and both of them proposed to you."

"It was complicated."

"No, it was simple, and you need not spare my feelings. Both of them found you lovely, and as it turns out, so did his descendant. We learned that one the hard way."

"The hard way?"

"Well, surely you must remember his ex-wife, Caroline Bingley." I closed my eyes.

"Blast it, did you meet her?"

"Oh yes," Elizabeth said, rolling her eyes. "And she mistook me for you and accused me of trying to get Mr. Darcy all that time while I lived here with them, blah blah blah."

"Oh no!" I covered my lips with my fingers. "Did she really do that?"

Elizabeth chuckled dryly. "Yes, she did. And I wanted to sock her into next year all the while. We both had to learn from Darcy's lawyer that she was the one who ruined the relationship because she cheated on him! What nerve of the damned woman to want to have a go at me for things that were entirely her fault! God the bum—"

"Face," she and I said in unison, and then we laughed together.

"Ah, so Caroline still did not change at all," I said as we had a good laugh later.

"Still has not. We still see her from time to time."

"Do you?"

"Yes, whether it's passing her on the street in the main parts of London, or because she always manages to find some reason to drop by here and give Darcy something else that she has found of his that she kept somewhere. The sordid minx."

"Well, I have news for you on that score."

"What?"

"There are two Caroline Bingleys."

Elizabeth's mouth fell open. "What?"

"There's a Caroline Bingley also in 1812. And they are the spitting image of each other."

"Seriously?"

"Yes."

"That is unbelievably stupid! That there are two of that woman? What, would it not have been better to have two of your sisters, or something like that? But nope! There were two Caroline bloody Bingleys. That's just cruel and unusual."

"Yes, it is. And I had to deal with both of those."

"Well, I am sorry in that way, because I just have to deal with one from time to time."

"But I can clearly see that it did not impede your progress with Darcy."

"It did not. No, only you did."

Surprised, I asked, "Pardon?"

"I do not mean for it to sound mean, but you must understand. It was hard for me to move from underneath your shadow."

"What do you mean?"

"Well, when Mr. Darcy arrived in London, he, well, it was no more than a few weeks after I had fallen into 1812, and I had just begun to settle in my mind that it was all a hallucination of some kind, that I had imagined falling into the past, when Darcy suddenly showed up right where I was."

"How did you both meet?"

Elizabeth blushed and she looked down once again.

"Well, it was quite funny."

"Was it?"

"He, uh, well, he suddenly appeared in my bathroom while I was taking a shower." She looked up at me. "He actually appeared in the shower."

"What?" I gasped, surprised beyond belief.

"Yes! There I was, taking a shower, and then there was a blast of light, water rushing everywhere, and he suddenly was standing there, getting very wet as I screamed. He gasped, apologized and called me Miss Elizabeth. I nearly fell out of the shower. I grabbed at all the nearby towels and then rushed against the door as he stumbled out of the shower stall.

"Then I realized that he was wearing the same clothes that I had seen when I had fallen into your time, and he kept saying my name over and over again. Rather than be afraid, I caught on really quickly, asked him how he knew my name and he looked confused, for he had always known it. Then he called me Miss Bennet, and I began to realize who he must have meant. I informed him that I was a different person, ordered him to stay in the bathroom while I got some clothes on, and then I came back with a newspaper to show him the date. Of course he did not take to learning that he had fallen into the future well, and he was quite beside himself for a time."

"And what was it like for you, for I can imagine that it was not easy."

"It is actually quite surprising how quickly one can adjust to insanity when one is accustomed to it or chooses to accustom themselves to it. I suppose I was able to adjust and overcome any fear of the sight of him in the matter of minutes, because he confirmed to me that I was not insane."

"Oh."

"Yes, just seeing him standing there, all wet, like I was once, and thinking he was in 1812, well, it made me feel better immediately, and only cemented what I knew was real. You can't quickly go back after undergoing such an experience, you see. I had only been in your time for a matter of hours, but I always wondered what happened, what was the fate of your sisters and who was the woman they mistook me for. I wondered about you every now and again. Then this man falls into my shower, named Mr. Darcy, and he is of your world, I am mistaken for you again, and he clings to me. I didn't have much of a social life, you see, before. I was so career-driven, which was good, but it does lead to a woman every now and again feeling starved. It was as if he fell out of the sky, you must understand."

I did feel sympathy toward her. "Yes, I can."

"And because I was the only one who would believe him, and I had undergone the same situation, he needed me always. I wasn't used to that, you must understand. I never had a man who just needed me always and depended on me."

She bit down on her lower lip and smiled. "I quite liked it. It made me feel helpful. At first that was all it was. I had a hard time getting him to believe that I was not you, and then there were pictures of him on the news, on the internet and all, declaring that he was missing, for he had not shown up to work for two weeks and because he had not also returned home.

"I convinced him to pretend that he was his descendant, because it would be nice to have a place and money of his own and also this way, his descendant's finances and house would not be lost in case he did return again. He agreed and I held his hand all the way through it, I led him into the station so that he could be identified, and would you believe it? Some git there just had to call Caroline and she came there, pretending to be all happy and then she saw me, and she freaked out. She started screaming at me in public, calling me Elizabeth Bennet, and that was when we discovered that not only did she think I was you, but also that you had fallen in time yourself."

She stopped a moment, apparently thinking. "This threw Mr. Darcy for a major loop. It took us quite a while to make any sort of sense of it all. And yet, due to us always having to cling to the little bit of knowledge that we had, always being tossed about by ignorance, we spent so much time together just trying to make sense of things."

"And that was when it began?"

"When what began?"

"When the two of you began to fall in love with each other."

"Oh, I wish. That was simply when I began to fall in love with him. But it perhaps took longer for him to fall in love with me."

Why did that make me feel a little better?

"You see, it was more than simply us always having to put our heads together and discover what happened to us, but it was also us learning about his descendant, and my ancestors. I found you in the family tree databases online. I found out when you lived and when you passed away."

Now, that shocked me! "You learned about when I died."

"Yes, it was in the year 1880 and—" she stopped talking immediately. "Oh, sorry of course you would not want to have known that."

"Yes, well, we all have to die sometime, therefore don't worry I am not afraid. But, did I marry Mr. Darcy? What did the family tree say?"

"Yes, it said that you did," she replied, bitter.

I sighed in relief, but then I noticed her expression.

"But why are you upset about that? I marry the Mr. Darcy that fell through time."

"Because his ancestor did not know that when he saw it. He did not know if it was his descendant or if it was he himself."

The comprehension dawned and I saw what she had meant. Both men had the same name, Fitzwilliam Darcy. Thus, if she had fallen in love with the one from 1812, and he saw that, he naturally would not consider her for a time, thinking it was his destiny to return and we would get married. Time had messed things up while also putting them to rights.

"Yes, I see." I rubbed my chin. "But it all came out right in the end, because you got married."

She shook her head. "Because he eventually gave up and I know that it was part of it. After a year of being here, he resolved on accepting that he would never return."

"But how did he make a living? I know that his family had a lot of money, but he could not live that way forever."

"Yes, I also helped him in that way too. When his job called him, expecting for him to return, he didn't want to go. So, I went with him, acting as if I was his new assistant, and I would learn about his job through others and advise him on how to do everything."

"You did all of that, for him?"

"Yes, but through it all, he still saw you when he looked at me. Well, you must understand, that hurts."

She wiped her eyes with a tissue. "When the ghost of another woman is looming over you, and the man cannot see who you are, well, I cannot describe the feeling. The world makes a mockery of people in our situation. They ridicule us for when we have a hard time moving on from things, but it's not so easy. When you meet that special one, you know he's perfect and you can't…"

"See yourself with any other," I finished for her.

"Precisely. I had never felt that way before. So, I could not just accept and move on so easily from him, and it took me a whole year of just being a companion to him."

I laughed a bit.

"What?" She grimaced at me. "Am I being funny?"

"Nothing at all, it is just that you reminded me of a character."

"What character?"

"Oh, you totally reminded me of the character Martha from Doctor Who!"

She stifled a laugh. "Oh, shut up! Besides I liked Martha."

"Oh, I did too."

"Oh, very well then, I was like her. And I'm not ashamed of it. So, don't you dare ridicule it."

"Not at all, I was in your situation a bit."

"Were you?"

"Yes, when I was stuck in this time period, I had to watch Darcy with Caroline Bingley, and then I had to go to their wedding and watch her walk down the aisle to a man who I was in love with. A bloody nightmare."

"Oh, that must have been murder."

"It was."

"Then, all that time and we were both in the same situation?"

"Yes, we were. We both had to watch them pine over a woman who was not us."

Elizabeth laughed, a sound that was familiar to me.

"And all that time, I despised you!"

"You did? Really?"

"Well, I had to hear him talk about how he proposed to you, how you had saved him, and how he had never met another woman like you before. And all this while I was always trying to help him with everything. Also so often he clearly was comparing me to you, or at least that was what I told myself. I thought that when he looked at me, he was just remembering. Just remembering the time where he came from, and the days he spent with you at Pemberly."

"I'm sorry that he did that. He perhaps didn't know the pain that he was causing you."

"Yes, but it never stopped it from hurting."

"But what changed it? What influenced you both to fall in love?"

"Oh, I eventually spoke up."

"You did?"

"Yes."

I leaned toward her. "What did you say?"

"I told him that I could not do it anymore. I told him that I could not stand there, always being beside him and with him never seeing me for who I was. I finally told him that I adored him, and that I thought he was beautiful. Yet because he would not see me for who I was, I didn't want to stay there, wasting my life as I waited for someone who would not value me in the way that I valued them. So, that was me…"

"Getting out," we both said in unison once more.

"Yup, I was getting out," she continued, "and then when I left his home, well, it was beautiful. Finally, I was standing up and choosing to move on, and I felt heaviness and a lightness that goes hand in hand with walking away from someone that will never love you in the way that you love them."

Elizabeth then got a faraway look in her eyes, as if she was recalling a bittersweet moment, which she was. Her voice grew soft and misty and I wondered if that was how I looked when I felt the emotion.

"Well," I prompted, "what happened?"

She smiled, almost shyly. "It was surprising, really, as I was leaving, he came after me. Would you believe it? All those hints I had been dropping throughout the year and he barely noticed them. I suppose he had spent so much time seeing someone else when he looked at me, that he never fully saw what I was feeling. And then he did it."

"What?"

"He decided to forget the past and try and see the present. And then we began to date as well as fall in love really quickly. We got married no more than a few months after I first asked him out. Perhaps no more than six months into the relationship, he proposed, and I very much was not at all in the mood to say no and be cautious, so we got married and it was a small and simple wedding. He likes small and simple things, despite having all the money in the world back in his time."

I placed my hand over hers.

"I am happy for you, Elizabeth." And I was.

She smiled gently and covered my hand with hers.

"To be honest, it was a bit of a wedding where I, well, when I married him, I was already pregnant."

I smiled at her. "Oh, one of those, huh? Well, that's fine too."

She laughed. "Yes, and I'm not upset about it, but I didn't tell him until after he had proposed, so he didn't feel pressured or anything. It turns out that he was happy to be a father so soon, but I'm not surprised, for coming from the time period he did, having a child was important. He's a good father."

"I am sure that he is."

"Yes, he is. Was. Is."

"He'll come back," I reassured her.

"Over time, I stopped hating you. And by hate, I mean, that I was no longer jealous of you, because I got what I wanted. He... he was the most beautiful thing that I had ever seen."

"I can understand that."

"And it all worked out in the end. Until now. And the children, well, what do I tell them?"

"Give your Mr. Darcy a month to return and if not, then we shall figure something out. Until then, we cannot risk your children discovering us."

"Oh," she confirmed bravely, "never fear, for I have thought of all that."

"You have?"

"I'm assuming that your Mr. Darcy still knows how to drive a car."

"I would imagine he does."

"Good." She handed me a wallet and a bag. "Tonight, find a hotel to stay in. There's my husband's debit and credit card in there. Don't worry; you know he has a lot of money on it. This is Mayfair, so your Mr. Darcy knows plenty of places in the area. And here," she said, handing me some keys, "take my husband's car. When he returns, of course you have to bring it all back."

"But I worry about us staying in a hotel for days upon end. I know Darcy has stacks of money and all, but I don't want him ringing up that much of a bill, and what about Darcy's business?"

"Well, you know how Darcy was. He has an office, but he can run much of his business from home, and you don't have to stay at a hotel of course."

At first, I did not understand, but then I read her expression.

"Oh!"

"Yes, you can return to Pemberly and stay there."

"Well, I'm happy to know that it is still in the family, but do you never go there with your children?"

"We do, but only in the summertime, so you have months there by yourselves before we have to figure something else out."

I brightened, happy with the good news. "Thank you, Elizabeth."

I stood up, preparing to tell the others when she grabbed my hand. "What is it?"

"This Mr. Darcy you are with now. You really love him, don't you?"

"Yes, I do. I always did. That was why I really never wanted to marry your husband, because I was already in love."

"Then I have nothing to fear in you being here."

"Elizabeth, not a damn bit."

She looked reassured. "Thank you."

I went back to the room that the rest of my company was stored, and it was the most amusing thing to see Jane, Kitty, Mary, Georgiana, and Zachary in the room, in modern day clothes, for they clearly felt very self-conscious.

I clapped my hands. "You all look brilliant," I offered.

"How do they wear these things though?" Kitty asked, referring to the jeans. "They are so restrictive."

"Now you know how we men always feel." Zachary chuckled and then he grew wistful. "Lydia would have laughed at that." Jane patted him on the shoulder.

I turned to Darcy, who looked handsome as ever in his original clothing apparel. He wore breeches very well, but always the custom 21st century trousers would always be his ideal style.

"You look beautiful," I acknowledged.

"And you had better know it," he replied, and we saw Zachary eye us with disdain.

"Oh, upon my word, get a chamber, you two. Seriously, we are stuck in the future, in a time that many of us don't comprehend, driven away from our families, and you still feel comfortable enough to flirt."

"This isn't our first time-travel adventure, Zach," Darcy said. "We've had time to adapt. And flirting is just a coping mechanism."

"Of course," Zachary replied shakily.

"Don't worry. I'll explain to you what a coping mechanism is later on."

"Good man, thanks. And why do you keep calling me Zach? Do not misunderstand me, I actually quite like it, but no one ever calls me that."

"It becomes traditional to call someone that when Zachary is their name. Also, it's from a TV show in the states, called 'Zach and Cody'."

All of them looked baffled.

"Don't worry. Elizabeth and I will explain what a TV show is later on too."

"Thanks," they said in unison.

"So, what do we do now?" Mary asked. "For I get the feeling that we cannot stay here."

"You're right. We cannot," Darcy said.

"And we will not," I confirmed, taking out the wallet and tossing it to him. I shouldered the bag and held up the keys. "Darcy, you've been gone for five years and yet you are still filthy stinking rich. And you also still have a car. Oh, and the best thing of all. You still have Pemberly."

Mr. Darcy gave me a gentle smile. "Oh, Lizzy. Of course I bloody well do!"

Chapter Nine

THE UNTIMELIEST NEWS

With sweaters or coats that had hoods, we left Darcy's old townhouse, and with it, we left all the memories of the past that I first had with him, and the fresh ones that we had just made. Yet as we all went to the car, I peered through the window and there I saw Elizabeth lifting up her daughter and twirling her around. As I did so, Darcy noticed where I was looking, and he followed my gaze.

"I wonder what she has to tell them," I explained what I was thinking, "about where their father is."

"We did not cause this, Lizzy."

"I know but look at them."

Elizabeth then picked up her other child and spun them both around in her arms, kissing their foreheads.

"Your ancestor. Those are his children."

"Yes, they are. I hope he is doing fine, back in his own time."

"Oh, if there is one thing that you Mr. Darcys' do better than any other man that I have met, it's that you are both very good at always coming back."

He gave me a sad smile. "True, true."

"Darcy, do you know what this means though?"

"What?"

"He had children here. It means that he can never go back. I mean of course he is back there now. But his life is here. He can never live a full life back in 1812. Because his life is now here."

"I had not thought of it that way," he confessed, "but it makes me wonder."

"What?"

"Where does that leave me?"

"Good question. Then again, I suppose that we don't really have control over that, now do we?"

"No, we don't. All we can do now is look after this lot." He gestured behind us at our family.

"Good point."

We then went to the car, while also explaining what a car was to our company, we entered, and I looked at Darcy as he sat behind the wheel.

"What?" I asked him.

"Well, it is just... I never thought I would get to drive one of these again." Darcy put the key into the ignition, started the car and we drove down the street. And he was happy once more.

※

We did not stay in Mayfair, but rather Darcy had recalled a place that he loved to stay in Kensington, for it had some of the better hotels there. As we drove through all the areas of London, Jane, Kitty, Georgiana, Mary and Zachary had their faces plastered against the windows of the car, soaking up everything like a sponge.

"This is what you saw when you first fell through time, Lizzy?" Georgiana asked.

"Yes, so when I woke up in the Delaware River in America, I suppose everything went up from there."

"Well, except for getting hit by one of these incredible contraptions," Jane said, looking at the car around her. "Lizzy, you really got hit by one of these things?"

"I did."

"Yeah, still sorry about that," Darcy apologized, and I patted his knee.

"That must have been horrible," Jane offered. "I am amazed that you survived it."

"So am I, but I suppose that one doesn't fall through time just to die from a car accident. That would hardly seem fair," I answered with a slight jocular air.

"And what is that?!" Georgiana gasped, leaning on the armrest, looking out the window.

"Oh, that is a double-decker bus," Darcy explained.

"Oh look!" Kitty pointed. "There is another one there. Can we ride one ever?"

"I'm sure that we can sometime."

Kitty stared out the window and sighed. "Oh, the Colonel would have loved this, but I shall not be sad, for I shall return to him. Yes, yes I shall."

She sounded as if she was attempting to convince herself and we all let her.

⊗⚜⊗

Eventually we arrived in the area of London called Kensington and we reached Darcy's hotel of choice and entered it. Since there were five of us women and two men, we had two rooms ordered for the women, one for Darcy and me, and one alone for Zach. Darcy and I separated, he was to explain how the plumbing worked in his room, and I to the women, who had a set of suites, so their rooms were joined by a bathroom that they shared.

And when I showed them the plumbing, they were amazed.

"Amazing," Mary cried when she saw the sink work. She ran her fingers over the fine marble. "It's just like magic."

"Yes, and this one is hot and the other is cold," I said, then I showed them the shower. While there were shower baths in our time, we did not have it at Longbourn, and even if so, shower baths in our time only gave out cold water, therefore, to do it with hot water was quite overpowering to their minds. Despite all that they had suffered, they could not help but be a little amazed by it all.

Straws were drawn and Kitty got to take the first shower; I showed her where the hotel soap and hotel shampoo was, and she went to town in there while we sat in the room and I showed them other things. Georgiana and Mary soon were conversing over their amazement of a lamp as they kept turning it off and on, and then they looked out of the window and down at the street.

"So, this is really London then?" Mary asked me as her eyes were all aglow. "Really, this is what London will turn into one day?"

"Yes, it stretches further than you can even see."

65

"London already was a world unto itself in our time," Mary said, "but now look at it. It's a universe."

"But what about America," Georgiana wondered. "We were at war with them. Did we win?"

I shook my head. "Sorry, we did not and now they are a country that is 51 states, I think. I could be wrong about that number though, but it's a lot."

"So, we did not get our colonies back," Mary said wistfully.

"I was sad about that as well when I first fell through time, but over time, you learn to be fine with it. Though every now and again I wonder what it would be like if history had been different. If time could be unwritten, and we had won. All those states, they are beautiful. I wish that we could still have them, but it's better this way, I suppose."

"You did see America?" Georgiana asked.

"A small part of it."

"And how was it?"

"Like I said, it was lovely. Just as London is. Georgiana, I know that you are experiencing difficulties now, but you don't need to worry. And nor do you, Mary. We shall return home, I promise, so look at this all as if you are going on holiday, but rather than simply taking a tour of the continent, you explored a different part of time and history. The world has greatly changed, and Britain is a sight to behold. And perhaps maybe we can even do more; we can visit China, Japan, South Africa…"

"South Africa?"

"Oh yes, or Egypt, or Canada. Believe me, it is all brilliant."

"Yes, well," Mary admitted, "I shall miss mother and father, but since you say that we shall return again, I shall not worry about that and besides, I did not really have much waiting for me back in our time."

I patted her on the shoulder and was about to make a move toward Jane when Georgiana grabbed my hand.

"Elizabeth?"

"Yes."

"Do you really think that I shall see my brother again?"

"I am certain that you shall."

"Very well, then I shall make the best of it. Though being in a new world presents dangers that one is not accustomed to."

"Of course," Mary said, about to cite a maxim, "because it is very well known, that the devil you know is always better than the devil that you don't."

Ah, dear Mary never changes. "Don't worry. Darcy will look after you all."

"And that's another thing," Georgiana stressed. "What is happening here? How can he and my brother look so much alike, and exist? How can Mrs. Elizabeth Darcy look just like you? This is too much of fate being facetious."

"While there could be something greater at work here, being in this era gave me time to learn things, and one thing is that names and faces get repeated. When it comes to family, names get passed down very easily. And in regards to facial features, there is even evidence in this time proving how two people, wholly unrelated, can look so very much alike. To the point of being identical."

I took a breath and continued. "The term is doppelganger, and since that is possible for two people wholly unrelated in the same time period, it is one hundred perfect possible and likely for different generations of the same family. So, this could all be fantastical, but it could also just be pure science."

"Can science explain time travel?" Mary asked.

"Oh, well, no it cannot."

"Then it's settled. This is fantastical."

Eventually I moved away from them and sat down next to Jane.

"Do you still miss Mr. Bingley?" I asked her.

"Of course. I did everything to catch him at last, and then at the beginning of the love of my life, what happens? I get whisked away into a journey that I suppose I will never fully understand or have the answers to. And yet I am not afraid."

"You are not?"

"No, because you are all with me."

I put my arm around her shoulders. "Dear Jane, your acceptance of this all is truly angelic and admirable."

"Oh, don't tease me, Lizzy."

"Indeed, I do not tease you."

"I do miss him terribly though, and time is most pernicious on us, for it has taken me from Bingley, and Kitty from the Colonel. And Lydia from Zachary. Also, it tore Georgiana from her brother for a long time now. Why is it doing this, I wonder? Why does it like us so much?"

"I don't know. All I can assume is one thing."

"And what is that?"

"That something was out of place to begin with, and it is just trying to set itself right somewhere."

"Then you think it made the mistake and is trying to figure itself out? Oh dear, I am now talking about Time as if it is a living breathing thing."

"I think it might be. Impossible things are happening every day."

"Well, this is your second time here, so I shall put my faith and trust in you, and my questions. Lizzy, I don't know if anyone asked this, so I shall. What was it like? Seeing the other Elizabeth there, the spitting image of yourself, and she was married to a man who you once were attached to."

"I admit that it was a shock."

She turned and gave me a long look. "Was that all that it was?"

"Well, I suppose that it was not so. It turns out, Jane, that she hated me."

"What?"

"She hated me for a time. Or at least, she loathed the very thought of me."

"Why?"

"Because she was in love with Mr. Darcy, the other one, and not mine, and he could not forget me so very easily. I never wanted him to fall in love with me, truly."

"I know."

"It was just something that sort of occurred randomly."

"You saved his life and then cared for him. Of course, he was going to fall in love with you."

I shrugged. "I was too busy trying to get everything in order to even notice for a time. And then I had made a mess of things."

"It was never your fault. Life just gets complicated, that is all."

"Thank you. I hope that one day she will look to see me with happiness. I want the two of us to get along."

"I am certain that you shall. And at least you still have Mr. Darcy with you."

I hugged her close again. "You shall see Mr. Bingley again, I promise."

"I hope that you are right," she said, looking sad. "Oh, Lizzy, I wanted him to so much be the first person that I told, and this all could not have come at a worse time."

"What do you mean by that?"

"Well, I really don't want to alarm you."

"What is it?"

"And please do not think of me during this all, for I shall be well."

"Jane, what is it?"

She looked down at her hands.

"Lizzy, I'm with child."

"You're pregnant?" I gasped, unable to believe it.

"Yes, I am."

Kitty emerged from the bathroom, interrupting the untimeliest news, covered in a towel and looking content.

"My Colonel would have loved this! Showers are brilliant! Bloody brilliant! Did I say bloody right? I heard Darcy say it and I just wished to use it."

Chapter Ten

BACK TO THE FUTURE

"Jane's pregnant?!" Darcy gasped as we lay in bed together.

"Yes, she is."

I had sat with Jane for a half an hour after she told me, but since Mary and Kitty were there to sit with her, I knew that Jane was fine, and she even wished for rest soon after I announced that I was leaving for bed. Once I got to the room, I told Darcy.

"Oh, good god, that is just so inconvenient," Darcy groaned.

"I know and poor Mr. Bingley, to be not present during this time. And poor Jane. This is not something she should be forced to bear, especially away from him."

"How far along is she?"

"She says that it is at least four weeks now. She wanted to wait until she made sure it was all certain before she told him. She didn't want to get his hopes up if it proved to not be the case."

"So, she is almost a month into the pregnancy?"

"Yes, which means that if we stay here for too long, then she will give birth here."

"As tragic as that is, there is one thing that she has in her favor in being brought to this time during her pregnancy."

"And that is?"

"Better maternity care. Nowadays, due to hospitals, women practically never die or suffer health side effects when giving birth. Perhaps that is why we are here. To make sure that Jane has a success in her first going into labor."

"That is a brilliant notion, but I think it is more than that. Either way, it is a good thought. With Jane being here, she shall be fortunate in that way. Makes me wonder if we ought to have a child in this era."

He laughed softly and pulled me to him. "With our luck, we'll fall back in time in your fifth month and then you'll hate me for it."

"Perhaps. Thank goodness we shall be going back to Pemberly, for that will be a perfect place for her to be for her lying in."

"It will. All roads lead back to Pemberly always, don't they?"

"Yes, they do, it appears. Georgiana is also no longer angry with you, by the way."

"I knew that she wouldn't be, for she was just upset at the news. And what about Kitty and Mary, how are they?"

"Mary is taking it perfectly, while Kitty is bearing it very admirably. She seems to have an inherent faith in us, she believes that she will see the Colonel again, and keeps reassuring herself of it."

"That is the best thing to do."

I turned to look at him. "And how about Zachary?"

"I left him when he was taking a shower. It seemed to make him very happy. Wait until I show him the television tomorrow. But what about you, Elizabeth? How are you right now?"

I felt so comfortable snuggling against him. "It is strange. I am sad to be returned, but also happy for it as well. It is clear that I missed my home when I was here, but I missed this all."

"Oh, so did I. Lizzy, I admit that I am happy to be back here in my time."

"I know, and I am happy for you. But wait, Pemberly still has indoor plumbing and all that?"

"Of course, don't be silly," he said with a chuckle.

"Just checking," I pinched his chest and he kissed my forehead as we fell asleep.

⊗

The next day, we woke up and Darcy had the good idea that we all ought to go shopping and get some clothes, since we did not wish to walk around in the same clothes all day. So, we went to inner city London, and went to the main shopping sites for clothes that were nice, that did not look too posh or as Darcy put it 'as if we were trying too hard'.

When we went there, we had to have help from the shop girls, who marveled at how we did not really know our clothing sizes, but eventually began to have fun with it. Eventually we all left that day with three pairs of pants, a skirt, a few shirts, a dress, and a coat while Zachary and Darcy walked away with some men's attire as well. We also had to get some shoes as well and eat, therefore by the time that we were done, we could not go to Pemberly, but had to return to the hotel.

All of my sisters kept on looking at their purchases for that day and marveling at the fashion of that era.

"I don't know if the fashion of this era is better or worse than ours," Kitty said, "but I'll give them this. At least they don't have to wear *stays* like we do, or any corsets of any kind."

"I quite like the clothing," Mary intoned, putting on a pair of her recently purchased pants. "It is nice and simple. I like simple as you know. And these are called jeans?"

"Yes, they are."

"Why did some of them have holes in them though?" Jane asked. "How did the sellers not notice that? I was afraid to ask, because I felt that I was being rude."

"No, that's actually the style, and those rips in the pants are fashionable to some."

"Ah, strange. But if it suits them."

Kitty picked up a shirt and twirled around with it.

"Oh, if the Colonel had seen me in this, his jaw would have dropped in shock. Which reminds me, when we fall back into time, I'm going to try and take some things with me. It would be nice to have proof of where we were."

I laughed at her enthusiasm. "Be careful, or you shall make sweater dresses become a creation long before it was expected."

"Oh, maybe that's why they get created," Kitty said, "because I couldn't leave things alone and brought it all about."

We all looked at each other in wonder.

What an idea! That Kitty Bennet could accidentally be the person who inspired sweater dresses to come into effect in the world.

The next morning, as I was in the bathroom brushing my teeth, I heard a phone ring, and Darcy picked it up. At first, I had thought that it was the hotel phone, and then I realized that it was a cell phone, and that he was speaking to Elizabeth, Mrs. Darcy.

I pressed my ear to the door and listened.

"Well, I wish that I could help," Darcy said in reply, "but I don't see how I could. After all, if I come over, then your children will definitely see that I am not their father and that there is something wrong."

There was a pause in the conversation as Darcy was listening.

"I will have to talk to Lizzy about this," he said in response about something, "and then I will call you back in ten minutes. I promise that I will. It is just, this is awkward."

Eventually the phone call ended, and I went out to see him as he turned to me.

"Sorry," I began, "I overheard a little bit of that."

"Oh."

"What does Elizabeth want you to do for her?"

"She wants me to go to her home for a few moments and pretend that I am her children's father."

My heart dropped. "Oh, dear god."

"Precisely, I would make a bloody mess of it all."

"I know, and yet I understand where she is coming from."

"Yes, but it is ridiculous, right?"

"Oh, it is, but come to think of it, what isn't ridiculous in all of this? She doesn't know when their father is going to return, and perhaps she has had a change of heart of it all, and she does want to see you, in order to make an appearance. She probably misses him."

"But I'm not their father." At this he was insistent.

"I know, but is there any way that it could be a quick visit? Could you tell them that their father has to take a holiday and shall return when he can? Like in about a month. Hopefully we shall be gone in a month."

"Gone?" Darcy blurted out, looking at me inquisitively. "Then you want to return back to the past?"

I blinked and then realized what I was implying.

"Oh, I think I did mean that. And you want to stay of course."

"Yes, I was hoping that maybe we both wanted it. After all, what can be better than this all? Come now, Elizabeth, you know that you love it in this era."

"I do, but the fact is that I have to think about other things. Haven't you noticed how I cause damage by being in this time?"

"How so?"

"Darcy, look at this? Here I am, in an era where my descendant looks just like me and I am affecting her life, perhaps in a negative way."

"Oh."

"And then I have my sisters I have to look after, my parents to return to, and also there is your ancestor to consider. He now has children here. Is there room for us here, or are we making this all feel as if it has become pretty crowded?"

"Oh blast it!"

We both sat on his bed and stared at the blank wall.

"I would like to stay here with you," I said, "but if we stay here, we have to wonder, what will happen to the past? And then there is something else."

"What?"

I rested my hand on his arm. "We have to consider this. I know that you shall hate me for suggesting it, but we have to."

"Well go on then," he replied stoically, "get on with it."

"We have to acknowledge, that if one set of us does not return, then there will be no Pemberly."

The thought was too devastating to consider for too long therefore after a while, Darcy saw the importance of going back to his old home and pretending to be his ancestor for a few moments. Therefore, I decided that it was best to go with him, with a hood over my head, trying to appear inconspicuous. I sat in the car while he knocked on the front door, and Elizabeth answered it. She saw me in the car, waved to me and then Darcy disappeared inside while I sat there, worrying over how it all went.

Darcy was not in there for more than a few moments before he emerged and had a laptop bag slung over his shoulder. He got back in the car and looked a little relieved.

"You look happy, so I am assuming that it had went well," I noticed.

"They were little; therefore it was not hard at all. It was just some hugs and promising that I shall see them soon, because I have to go on a trip."

"Oh, that's good."

"And Mrs. Darcy gave me this," he said, gesturing to the laptop. "After all, I'm going to need this for resuming work at Pemberly."

"That's true. It was nice of you to help."

He started the car again.

"Just happy to be back," he said, "now let's get the rest of them and start heading to Derbyshire."

We drove back to Kensington, picked up our family and then we drove out of London.

Our ride out into the country was pleasant, most pleasant in fact, and then once more I found myself looking at the new Pemberly, as I had done some time ago.

"It gives me hope," Georgiana said from the backseat. "Pemberly is still the same, therefore all feels well."

We entered Pemberly, and while it was nice to return, Georgiana looked down as she noticed a change here and there, accommodating the present that it was in.

"That's a phone, isn't it?" she asked us, looking at a phone on the table.

"Yes, it is."

"That would have made our parents angry."

We all chose our guest rooms and what Georgiana was not upset about was the plumbing, for when she saw the bathrooms, she was overjoyed.

"Oh, sitting in that car has made me long for a shower, so that would be brilliant."

Darcy and I let them settle in while we travelled to the nearest supermarket to get food for the house.

"Can you cook at all?" I asked him.

"A bit."

"Good because I learned how to cook a few dishes when I worked as a nanny. Hopefully with our heads together, we can always cook some meals to last the week."

"Works for me. Elizabeth?"

"Yes?"

"What if... what if we never get the chance to go back? What if we are stuck here?"

"This history will change again," I concluded. "After all, Mr. Darcy will have to remarry to have an heir."

"Oh, I had not thought of that."

"But you were right. Let's not worry about this now. Let's just buy some eggs."

We all settled into Pemberly very well. Between having to adapt to modern times, and learn about the world, our family was most preoccupied.

And then Jane's pregnancy grew over time and we had to occupy ourselves with seeing that she had care. Darcy was kind enough to find a way to give her health insurance, we found doctors for her in Derbyshire, and then it all began to feel a little too real.

"We have been gone for a month now." Jane sighed as Darcy was taking her to the maternity doctor one day. "I know you said that time moves differently than it does for us, but I cannot help but fear that it won't. I know I must sound like a repeated gif on the internet, but I worry that Mr. Bingley will forget all about me."

I chuckled at her remark towards the internet, because it did in fact show how far we had come since our arrival. Between Darcy having internet chat meetings, he and I got our family acquainted with all the 21st century luxuries. Zachary was a very strange sort of a situation, because he feared change so very much. He liked the advancements made in plumbing, but the computer concept frightened him for the longest time, and he scoffed when we showed him a cell phone, labelling it as positively diabolical.

"A voice that comes through the phone!" he had remarked. "That is just monstrous! Really, we have all gone too far now. I can enjoy the television, because it is bang on, and is quite educational, but that's as far as it goes. And who would have thought that I would miss my breeches?"

"That's just bloody strange," Darcy had noted. "How could any man miss those?"

"They flattered my legs more. In this era, it is hard to get a pair of trousers that suit your legs. Whoever designs them makes them tight in all the wrong places."

Over the course of their stay, we had to make sure that we were clear what to believe on the tele versus what was fiction or downright fantasy. Yet once we threw 'Lord of the Rings' and the 'Hobbit' films into their lives, there was really no going back for them. Their curiosity was seized, and even the deepest desires and attachments to 1812 began to wane, and all that was missing from their lives were our families. Time had opened their eyes, and I worried that they would not be able to adapt whenever we did return back to the time we had come from. Falling back into the past had once taken a toll on me, and I wondered if it would be worse for them. Especially for Mary and Georgiana, who had no romantic ties.

At least with Zach, Kitty and Jane, their hearts were still yearning across the years for what they left behind, but with the other two it could easily be different, and only time would show me how strangely correct that I would be.

❧

Jane's fragile state was something she bore very well, but with her altered state, came the natural tendencies of a pregnant woman. She grew anxious sometimes, nervous and sometimes paranoid. There were times where Kitty told me that she had to sleep in Jane's room, holding her, because she had fits of loneliness. At first, I felt a little insecure why Jane went to Kitty before me, but then I realized that our relationship had changed. I was no longer just her sister, but Mr. Darcy's wife, without fully holding that title, and she did not wish to interrupt it.

Thus began our lives, and once more we were back to the future.

Chapter Eleven

TANGLED

O ne day, at breakfast, Georgiana turned to Darcy and me.
"Elizabeth and Fitz," she announced, "Mary, Kitty and I were talking."

We looked at Kitty and Mary, who also nodded.

"This all feels slightly ominous," Darcy observed.

"Oh, it's nothing bad."

"Oh, brilliant. Sorry, I am just so used to someone being angry when they say that they were talking."

"Well, it is just…I was wondering…might we get our own laptops?"

"And perhaps we should all get a phone," Mary added. "This way we can keep track of each other better."

"Oh, no, we shouldn't get those blasted things," Zach said, "for I feel as if those would eat our minds."

"Oh, for the last time, Zach, they are not evil," Darcy explained.

"You don't know that."

"But we really ought to," Mary stressed, "for now that we have gotten used to this world, I feel as if we ought to go out and see it. More closely."

"Well, I'm not against it," I said.

"Me neither," Darcy said. "Well tomorrow, let's go to the phone department in the retail park that's in Lambton, for there are a lot of shops and there should be an AT&T place."

"Good, thank you; that would be delightful."

The next day, when Darcy had finished a morning meeting, we all went to the retail park in the Lambton village, which held the phone store, along with a slew of other quaint stores nearby, even included a store called, 'Books and Beyond!'

We had entered the phone store, and the customer service people were shocked and a little alarmed that we requested phones that had no internet on them, for we had not known that there was no longer an option at all. But luckily, flip phones were back in fashion, due to them being now regarded as 'retro', and I recommended them, for they were least likely to break easily.

"I feel as if I am going to drop this at any moment," Kitty said, looking upon hers.

"Don't worry," I explained, "they are stronger than you may think."

"But what does it mean?" Mary asked the customer service woman. "Unlimited texting plan?"

The woman flinched. "Oh, well, it means that you get unlimited texts for this amount of money."

"Right, right. Yes, good, good."

Pause.

"And what are texts exactly?"

"We'll take the plan," Darcy said to the woman and then he whispered in Mary's ear, "I'll explain later."

"Thanks," Mary whispered in reply, catching on.

When we walked out of the store, we passed the bookstore and a sign caught Mary's eye.

HELP WANTED
NOW HIRING

"What does that mean?" she asked. "Or does it mean what it would mean in our time? That they are hiring people?"

"Yes, it does," I said, looking at the bookstore. Then I looked back at Mary, whose expression was curious. "What?"

"Oh, nothing," Mary answered. "It is just, we've been here for over a month and I feel as if I got a handle on things. And I hate sitting at home, doing nothing, and not helping at all."

"Mary, you don't need to feel useless."

"But I do. I always did, you know. But what if I…"

"Mary, are you looking to get a job?"

"I am admittedly thinking about it. What do you think?"

"I admit that usually people prefer you to have some business in retail before you apply, but we'll see what we can do. Come on, let's go in and get an application for you."

"What do you mean by an application?" She followed me in.

"Don't ask that question when you speak to the person at the desk. Just say, 'Hello, I read the sign in the window and was wondering if I could fill out an application'."

"Right. Could you repeat that all again?"

I repeated it and then we walked up to the desk, where we were met by a really prudish woman who seemed to think she was too good to work in a bookstore, and it made me realize why they perhaps would need to find new people.

Mary rose to the occasion, she was given an application, and when we emerged from the store with the application, all of our company looked on us.

"Buy a book?" Darcy asked.

"No, I just decided to embarrass myself," Mary said. "I am…going to try and apply for a job."

"Ah. Seriously?"

"No need to sound surprised, my love," I whispered to him.

"Oh, right. Right. Sorry, good for you, Mary."

Mary looked a little shaken. "Do you think I am being foolish?"

"No," he blurted out, "it's not that. It is just, I am surprised is all. You see, I am surprised that you would want to work, because from the world you are all from, you are not expected to."

"I see what you are referring to," Mary said, "but while the freedom from manual labor is a luxury of our station back home, it was not the freedom I ever sought, you see. In fact, it is the freedom to do things that I wish to do, which was something I always wished to aspire to. And well, I wish to be doing something now. In fact, I always wish to be doing something, but I never really had the chance. There are little choices for a middle-class woman in our time. Either we marry, or we don't, and that is all."

"Oh, yes, I did notice that."

"I just had no idea that it had such a profound effect on you," Jane noted.

"No one seemed to notice really," Mary confessed. "After all, there seemed to be not much room for me anywhere."

We all looked at each other and knew not what to say, but there seemed to be no concept of what to say. Mary was being very naked in revealing her true feelings, and when a person does that, they expose all around them and then there is a feeling of unease. It is important to undergo, but it just leaves one not knowing what to say.

"Well," Georgiana said, smoothing over our silence, "you want to get a job? That's brilliant, and you're braver than I am, I declare."

Mary blushed. "I have no experience. Therefore, I hope that I am not just wasting my time in this attempt."

"Well, there's never a way of really knowing," I elaborated. "I was quite rubbish at being a nanny when I first started working as a babysitter. It took me three whole weeks to get the hang of things. Now that I think about it, I can't understand why they didn't fire me really. Oh sorry, that was not much of a pep talk, now was it?"

"Oh, it's fine," Mary assured me, smiling. "If anything it makes me less afraid now. If you could have gone through all that, then I know not to be so hard on myself."

۞

We returned to Pemberly and while I had never worked in a shop before, luckily Darcy had. Despite being born rich, his mother had made him get a few shop-boy jobs when he was in school, hoping it would help him not be spoiled. So, he was able to give Mary some pointers. He told her that if she got hired, then it would be best to take notes while she was training so that she would be able to understand how to work the cash register quicker.

He also was willing to do the wonderful thing of letting her lie on her application and say that she was an assistant to an employee of his back in London once, and thus Mary had to be taught how to work Word processing systems on the computer as well. She also began to research popular authors of our time so that she could strike up a cord with people.

She also was given a Kindle device so that she could read books quickly and order them whenever she wanted, to improve her knowledge of pop culture and modern book trends.

One day she professed to me, "Despite it all," she said as she read, "I like many children's books in this time period more than anything else. I quite like these chapter book ones called Berenstein Bears, for they are simple and I can read them quickly. But some of the adult books are too graphic for me, and I'm going to need more time in this era before I shall be able to read them."

Mary had been resolved, and then she in fact did hand in the application. I had escorted her, for she would need to learn how to take the bus there and back if she were to work, and therefore I did my best to adjust her to public transit.

"I love the bus," she cried, when we were returning from our outing, riding from Lambton for the bus had a stop a few blocks away from Pemberly. "This way, I can be more independent without the fright of learning how to drive. Lizzy, I do not ever think I could master the idea of driving a car."

"I never did either when I first came to London," I allowed her to know, and as we sat there, I noticed a change in her. From her fitted coat, her total embracing of a warm pair of UGG Boots, to her letting her hair fall down with a knitted hat over it, I could not help but realize that her looks were greatly improved. "Mary, if you do not mind me saying, but your looks are very much enhanced, and I believe you look quite lovely."

"Really?" Mary blushed, running her hand over her hat. "Yes, at first I thought I would hate wearing these jeans, but I quite like them. And I like UGGs. I know they are not considered lovely, but I like them a lot. And the coat, hats and all that. I also like being allowed to wear my hair down."

She looked pensive. "It's...I miss our family, yes, but I admit that I actually am having a good time here. After all, there is nothing for it, we are stuck here, and I figure that I gain nothing by pining about the past."

"You are right to do so and...Mary, forgive me if I did not read this all correctly, but being here, in this time, it seems to be doing you good. Is it me, or did you need even further distance between yourself and Mr. Collins?"

Mary bit her lip and cracked her knuckles.

"Oh, don't do that," I said, cringing.

"You are right, sorry. It is just this thing I keep seeing people do and I know it's a bad habit, but it's so addictive. Yes, in truth, Lizzy, it is so. I feel that, since we are so far away, there is no way that I can see him. Back in our time, the possibility of witnessing Charlotte and him loomed over my head, like a frightful shadow that would rise up and engulf me.

"Yet here, I am not running, because there is no need to run. I am free from it all." She threw her arms in the air, strictly a motion the old Mary would never do.

"Also, being here now, I have come to this revelation that all those things we left behind, well, they are so small now. Even Lady Catherine feels small under the weight of the universe. All of her cares, her considerations, all the small things that we care about seem so meaningless."

She turned to me, her expression bright. "Elizabeth, we all spent so many years worrying about getting married, for we would have no futures, and we should not have been made to endure that sort of weight over us. Why were we not allowed to have more to think about? Things are all tangled now, but I feel as if it clears certain things up. Well, now I have more to think about, and it is quite lovely."

Eventually we returned to Pemberly.

Chapter Twelve

THE DATING LESSONS

"I got the job!" Mary cried when she got off her cell phone. It had been a week since she had handed in her application, she had come from her interview two days before, and clearly the bookstore had gotten back to her about it.

"I cannot believe it!" she cried as we embraced her. "I actually got the job!"

"Oh, that is wonderful," Georgiana said. "How about we all go to support you on your first day and buy some books?"

"I would love that, thank you Georgiana," Mary said, and her happiness gave her cheeks even more pretty rosy color. "Oh, can you believe it? I hope I am good at this! What if I fail? No, never mind, I cannot think that way. No, mustn't think that way. Oh, but I have never read any of the 'Game of Thrones' books. Everyone knows about those, so is that bad? Wait, no, people usually just watched the show, and the books are read every now and again or something like that."

"Don't worry," Darcy offered, "just try not to get nervous and do your best. But forgive yourself when you make a mistake, because hating yourself only makes things worse."

"Thanks, and I wish I wasn't so nervous," Mary rushed out, "but there is nothing I can do about it, it seems. Being nervous is aggravating. And it's rubbish."

"What is all this about?" Zachary said as he entered the dining room where we were all sitting. "You all look happy for a set of people who are still caught in the wrong time."

Not to anyone's surprise, Zachary was the last one who was still having a hard time adjusting to the 21st century, so he rarely smiled.

"Oh, Mary got the job at the bookstore in Lambton," Kitty explained, "and we are planning to visit her on her first day."

"The bookstore, right, right, right."

Pause.

"What exactly are we talking about again?"

☙❧

Mary was beginning her first shift after being trained. "Oh, this bookstore," Zachary said, sounding a little bored as we were all at Books and Beyond Store. She was at the register of the store, and Kitty was purchasing a copy of the books named 'Tumbling' and 'Leaving Cecil Street', which she had seen recommended on book websites.

"Well, Miss Bennet..."

"Zachery, you can call me Mary, you know." Mary smiled, giving Kitty back her change from buying the books. "I have it written on my name tag and everything."

"Yes well..." He sighed, but Jane, seeing how forlorn he was, took his hand and this calmed Zachary down somewhat. Zachary licked his lips in slight embarrassment over appearing ungentle, when we were interrupted by a man who came out of the back door. He was tall and lanky with a head of beautiful blond curls, cut short over his scalp. And, quite good looking.

"Mary, a shipment of books arrived and now it's time to learn how to unload them and enter them into the system." The man, who clearly was her manager stopped when he saw us.

"Oh, Tom," Mary said with a smile, "this is my family. They came to support me and the store for my first day."

"Look," Kitty said, "I just bought some books."

"Good choices," the man replied, smiling gently at her and her selection of books. "I am happy that you all came out to support Mary, and I think she shall be a good edition to the Books and Beyond Family."

"And how large is this family?" Georgiana asked, smiling. "Did you inherit the business?"

"I did." The man blushed when she smiled at him, and then he bit his

85

lip. "It belonged to my parents and while I hated inheriting it when I was younger, I've grown to be fine with it."

"These are my sisters Jane, Elizabeth and Kitty," Mary introduced. "And this is Mr. Fitzwilliam Darcy, and his sister Miss Georgiana. And this is their cousin, Mr. Zachary Fitzwilliam. Family, this is my manager, Tom. Tom Clarkson."

"Nice to meet you all," Tom said, his eyes constantly shifting to Georgiana. "So, you are the Darcys who are returned to Pemberly."

"Yes," Georgiana said, "we are."

"Yes, that place is often empty, but we've always heard great stories about it, here in Lambton." Then he turned to Zachary Fitzwilliam. "So, are you the owner of Matlock? When last we heard that place was just a museum now. Or are you all coming to live in it again?"

When he said this, Zachary's eyes widened.

"Matlock?"

"Yes. Oh, then you are not from that family? Sorry, I just assumed."

"No, I am," he nearly sputtered, "but I'm a distant relative, you see," Zachary rushed out. "And I don't know much about the family in this part of Britain. So, Matlock is a museum?"

"Well, it's more so a place where people pay to tour it."

"Because it's one of the few great homes in this side of England," Georgiana finished for him, coming to the point herself.

"Yes," he replied, looking at her significantly. "Though Pemberly deserves to always be the main house in Derbyshire."

"So, you've seen both homes there?" Georgiana asked.

"I used to run every day to the grounds of Pemberly when I was a boy," Tom pointed out. "I just liked running."

"I did too when I was a child. I used to like to run to Lambton a lot when I was a little girl. There was one brilliant tree that I used to like."

"Oh the green, by the landmark smithy shop," Tom offered.

Her eyes brightened. "It's still there?"

"Yes, yes, it is."

She laughed and clapped her hands. "I should not be surprised because it's a tree and they can live for centuries."

"Yes, this tree is old as hell. It must be from the 1700s or something. Can you imagine being that old at all?"

Georgiana's expression faltered, but she recovered.

"No, I cannot. But those are the drawbacks of being human, huh?"

"Yes, yes, they are."

"But does anyone know why Matlock is now simply a museum?" Zachary asked Tom. "Why wouldn't the family live there?"

"Well, I don't know for sure, but it doesn't really make sense in our times to be having such a bloody large house like that. No offense or anything," Tom said to Georgiana. "Like I said, Pemberly is brilliant, it is just—oh, sorry if I offended you."

"You did not offend me." Georgiana gave him a bashful laugh.

"Good. Good. Because I very much didn't mean to."

The poor lad! He had no idea how to flirt!

"Yes, well, Matlock, man!" Zachary urged.

"Right," Tom continued. "Well, the children of the last set who owned it did not feel like keeping it up, so they allowed it to be a place that people could visit to see those fancy homes, you know. Posh and all."

"The Fitzwilliams no longer live there?"

"No, it's just a fancy home on the other side of Derbyshire."

Tom looked insecure as Zachary stared at him in wonder, and then Zachary turned to Darcy.

"You never told me this."

"Well, it's because I am not that close to much of the family, so it did not occur to me."

This declaration startled me, and then it brought back an old memory from long ago—back to the first time that I had fallen through time and met Fitz. We had been discussing our families and confessing the inadequacy that we had felt with certain family members in it. I had spoken of Jane and he had spoken of...

"Let's go home now," Kitty interrupted, "for Mary has to start her day."

"Right," Jane said, putting her purchases in her bag. "Mary, promise me that you'll be safe riding home."

"They worry about me," Mary explained to Tom.

"A great family then," Tom said, smiling at Georgiana, who blushed and looked down at her feet, until they were interrupted as Darcy grunted, overprotective.

"Yes," I said hurriedly, "let's go."

"Did Fitz really just grunt when that man spoke with me?" Georgiana whispered to me as we travelled home.

"I believe that he did."

"I was just talking to him, that's all."

"And you both were just flirting."

Georgiana blinked. "We were just being cordial."

"And you were flirting. Don't worry; it's not bad in this time. In fact, usually men prefer it if you flirt with them first."

"What?" Georgiana gasped. "Surely they do not."

"Oh, they very much do. In fact, they prefer it if you make the first move sometimes. Well, in Britain yes, but I'm not certain about other parts of the world. He was quite attractive, this Tom Clarkson, wasn't he?"

Georgiana blushed again.

"Did you like him?" I cooed.

"I just met him."

"And did you like him?"

Georgiana laughed softly. "I…I suppose I am being stupid. But do you really believe that he liked me?"

"Georgiana, he smiled at you often and then stared at you when he thought no one was noticing. But I give you leave to like him, for you have liked many a stupider person."

"Dear Lizzy. Yet it does not matter. After all, one should not care for men here, since we cannot begin anything."

"Why ever would you not?"

Georgiana looked at me curiously.

"Because we will eventually return home of course, so I cannot marry someone here."

I blinked, having to recall how quickly the female mind in our time turned to marriage.

"Georgiana, I suppose I never mentioned this before, because I never thought there was any need, but the times are different here in that regard.

"You've seen it on the television. You date in this time. It's like a courtship, but there is nothing at all definite. At all. Truly, mark the words more than anything. You date someone, and if you do not like them as you thought, you apologize, but tell them that you do not wish to continue the relationship."

Her eyes widened. "And that really is it?"

"Yes. Of course, they can always tell you that they are not wishing to continue the relationship, and when that occurs, that means that they dumped you. And I've been told that it hurts a lot."

"It sounds like it does," Georgiana noted, her voice filling up with trepidation. "Oh, that would be most dreadful. So, he would break up with me, then?"

She covered her mouth when she realized that she had revealed too much.

"Oh, so your mind is already there, I can see?" I laughed.

She lowered her gaze. "I know it shouldn't be."

"Well, since you are here, you might as well accept that there is no need to put your life on hold for fear of marriage because that is not how things are done in this time. I suppose, well, we have to talk about boys now."

"No we don't!" Darcy shouted as we sat with Georgiana in his study. When we had returned, I told him that we should speak with her in private. Jane and Kitty were quite out of danger, for they were attached, but we had no idea that Georgiana would have to worry about relationships in her time, for the thought had never crossed our minds. "We don't have to think about this at all."

"Oh, Darcy, don't be obtuse about it," I argued. "Look at her, she's at the age for dating and men will look at her."

"They will?" Georgiana said, her interest piqued.

"Yes, they will," Darcy said, "and you shouldn't care about them at all."

Georgiana and I blinked at him, because we didn't believe that even he knew what he was saying.

"Darcy," I voiced, trying to suppress a smile, "are you being protective now?"

"Well I…" His voice trailed off.

"Well, I suppose that I am. Either way, it doesn't matter, because any day we could be pulled into the past again. Why should she start something that cannot be finished?"

"Because this may be her chance to live a little. Let's be honest, Darcy, we women don't get the chance to live much in 1812, because we are expected to grow up too fast. This will be good for her."

"I know but…well, this just doesn't seem like a good idea." He was clearly uncomfortable.

"Nothing is certain or anything. And no one has ever asked her out, but we ought to prepare her. If you tell her about what men are like in your time, it shall help her to understand."

"I know but—"

"But you are acting like my brother," Georgiana interrupted, "even though you are not."

We both looked at her suddenly and I marveled that she would say such a thing.

"Georgiana!" I gasped.

"Forgive me, but it is true."

There was silence between us, and Darcy felt so embarrassed, and I was not in the mood to stand by and let him feel ashamed because of the situation that he was forced into. Therefore, I suddenly grew protective and decided to speak for him. Again.

"Fine then," I declared. "If you are not going to be appreciative enough, and be dismissive, then you can go, and never mind."

Georgiana opened her mouth and then closed it. "I didn't mean…"

"No, it is fine. Go then!" I turned away.

"I just wanted to—"

I whirled back toward her. "To what? To hurt the man who fell through time and did his best to be the replacement of your brother. Do you think it was easy for him? No, it was difficult. He had to run an estate where he didn't know the duties of, he had to save my sister from a libertine, he allowed you to find your voice, and then we fall through time again, and he finds a way for us."

She appeared contrite. "I know and I realize that what I said was harsh."

"Yes, it was. Your brother is not here; therefore let this man do his best. He's your brother now, so treat him like one."

"I know." Georgiana looked up at Fitz. "I am sorry, really I am. I don't know why I said that. I am happy that you are protective of me, really, but it is just that you are letting it all get in the way of advising me on things. I don't know if I am ready for dating." Georgiana took a deep breath, choosing her words carefully, as if they were hard to say. "But if I am to be here, then I am here. Help me be here then, and don't hide me from the world. He did that very often. My real brother, I mean, and it led to me once almost consenting to an elopement. I was too shielded from things, and so… I love my brother tremendously, Fitz, but you are not him. Therefore, please, care for me, but don't hide me away from things."

When she finished her speech, I softened, and I saw Darcy's jaw relax.

"I suppose that I can see what you mean," he said.

"But still respect him," I magnified. "Just to be clear."

"Yes."

"Good." I brightened, sitting down beside her. "So let's begin. I didn't date much when I was in the modern day, because I fell in love with yours truly, but I met many women who did date. And while nothing can teach you better than learning from your own mistakes, I did the best I could to learn from them to the best of my ability. First thing's first: don't waste your time on liking someone who does not like you in return."

"That's easier said than done," Darcy commented. "But that is very true. Georgiana, if you do wish to present yourself out into the world, then you will eventually fancy someone who does not feel the same way. If they don't, don't do that thing that's popular in stories and keep on liking them, in hopes that they will eventually fall in love with you. It's a waste of your time, emotions and it drives you mad."

"Have you ever done that?" Georgiana asked and her question hung in the air for a moment.

"Yes," Darcy said at last.

Georgiana gave him a sad smile. "Well, as you know, I have been there as well, and you know as well as I do, that often there is nothing that can be done. We all simply have to feel what we feel. Therefore, don't worry. I know how it feels already."

"Very well," Darcy continued. "Now, here are some very simple rules.

"One: If he says that he will call you, and he doesn't, don't care about him. Period. If he says that you should always call him, then he is the worst and just don't speak to him again. Because not only is he showing that he does not care about you, but he's so high on himself that he honestly thinks you should be the one to make the moves on him and he doesn't have to do anything.

"Two: If he has a car, then he picks you up. If he always tells you to take the bus to see him, don't speak to him ever again.

"Three: If he goes out with you and doesn't eventually offer you anything real, you are not being paranoid for thinking he really doesn't care, because he doesn't.

"Four: If it is clear that he is not as interested in you as you are in him, or if he has many bad qualities, then don't wait around hoping for him to get better or think you can change him. No woman can change a man if he doesn't see that he has anything wrong with himself. Also, no woman can change a man at all. He has to want to change himself, and if he does not, then he does not want to change at all.

"Five: if he is not loyal to you, just leave. Do not remain with a person only so they can keep on hurting you. Honestly, what's the bloody point?

"Six: If he doesn't have a job, reconsider dating him. Not because of financial difficulties, but because mostly men's identities are wrapped up in their professions. You don't want to date someone who is suffering from an identity crisis; they'll use you like you're their tourniquet, and then you both will get hurt.

"Seven: Never, EVER, date a man who never believes he is wrong. I dated women who thought they were never wrong, and when you do, they will always justify treating you like rubbish, because they've always gotten away with it.

"Eight: Never date someone who is very smart and knows it; they have no sense of humility, and because of such, they can't see when they are doing something thoroughly stupid. Men who are not that smart, and know they are not, are actually the wisest men to be with sometimes; they don't use their intelligence to justify being abusive."

Georgiana listened with rapt attention, but to my surprise, Darcy continued on and on, and the list was almost endless. Indeed, the only reason that he stopped speaking was because Jane said it was time for dinner.

That being said, when Georgiana left us, she kissed him on the cheek and gave him a look of incredible admiration.

※

Later that evening, after we had been intimate, Darcy and I lay in his bed, in an embrace as he ran his hands down my bottom and stroked my thighs.

"Absolutely amazing." I laughed, kissing his chin.

"What?"

"Oh, nothing so little, so great, or sensible. It is only that, well, you had a lot to say today. And all of it was very correct."

"Yes, I did go on a lecture, didn't I?"

"You should write a book. But still, what I mean when I say amazing is that when men complain about us women not communicating or about us being the problem in the relationship, you men are criticizing each other, telling us not to speak to a man at the slightest provocation, and then you create the very miscommunication problems that you hold in disdain."

"Ah, I know! It is so strange, and it seems hypocritical, but it is almost as if we have no choice really."

He lifted himself up on one elbow. "You see, it is always best to tell us what you feel, but here is the thing: when a man cares, he acts a certain way, just as when if he doesn't care, then he will also not act a certain way. But we worry that if we tell you to talk to him, that he is going to do that painful thing, that awful thing, of telling you that you are paranoid, he is going to argue with you until you believe him, even when he knows you are correct."

He flipped onto his back again. "People, by nature, don't want to lose arguments, and we very much don't. Therefore, we don't want to risk the girl getting smacked down by a man who doesn't care and then he gets mad about it when she realizes this. Therefore, it's better that we tell you to not talk to him so that you don't get tricked. He'll only confuse you, then you will do something insane or that you will regret."

"Then I suppose that miscommunication shall always exist," I summed up.

"I know it's hard, but honestly, there probably always will be miscommunication, because we men are simply trying to protect you."

"An honorable thing," I nibbled his chin. "Chivalry isn't dead."

"Do you really think Georgiana will date, though?" he asked sincerely.

"Are you worried that she will?"

"I suppose that I am. I still have to protect her, and her brother would hate this."

"He would. But like she said, maybe this all is a bridge that she has to cross. I'm beginning to wonder if this whole situation was larger than us the whole time."

"What do you mean?"

"I mean that our actions were like ripples, and they affected many things."

"Like a butterfly flapping its wings… that sort of effect?"

"Yes, that sort. By all this occurring, Georgiana's path was changed, as was Jane's, Kitty's, Lydia's, and Mary's. I don't see what Zachary has to do with this all, but still. Maybe Georgiana was the one who needed this world. She needed to be allowed to do more than what she would have done."

"It is possible, I can say that, but you see, you are missing the big picture."

I raised an eyebrow. "Oh, am I?"

"Yes, you are."

"And what is this big picture?"

"How we were earlier."

"Pardon?"

Darcy's eyes grew misty as he ran his fingers from my bottom, to in between my thighs and began to rub me gently.

"The way we were together," he continued, "when Georgiana almost offended me, you supported me there, you defended me, and you were brilliant. I liked how we were a team."

"Yes, we were, weren't we?" I sighed, breathless from him rubbing me in my intimate spot. "You see, that's the real problem, you see?"

"What is that problem?"

"I love you terribly."

"As do I with you."

We made love once more.

Chapter Thirteen

MATLOCK UNDONE

As a team, we went downstairs the next day, and since we had long since hired a cook for the place, we were all sitting down for breakfast; all but Zachary.

"Where is he this morning?" Kitty asked.

"No idea," Georgiana said. "But it may be best that he is left alone for a time. I could tell that he was getting even angrier than before."

"I was hoping for the opposite," Darcy confessed, "for this is getting tedious. Don't get me wrong I know he's upset but…"

"No, I can understand," Mary said. "We can't improve our situation therefore he needs to improve."

"If only Bingley had been brought forward through time and not him," Darcy said, but then Jane looked up abruptly and caught his eye. "Oh, sorry."

Jane's glance dropped to her stomach. "No need to be. I wish it could have been that way as well."

"I didn't mean to make you sad."

"No, it's fine," she rushed out. "Truly it is."

We were silent for a moment, but luckily, we were interrupted when we heard Zachary's familiar footsteps. When he entered, we all looked up at him and he froze.

He gave us a smirk. "What? Sorry, did I alarm anyone by being late for breakfast? Blast it, it's not like we are back in 1812, or anything."

He sat down and served himself some food, and we all watched him uneasily. He felt our eyes on him and looked up.

"What?"

Except for Georgiana, we all shrugged our shoulders and looked down at our plates and continued eating.

"I think you want to talk about something," Georgiana blurted out, to which we all couldn't help but flinch at. "Zachary, am I wrong?"

Zachary looked up at her and then around at us at the table, one by one.

"Ah, you've been talking about me."

"Zach," Jane said, "it is just, well, we are a little concerned."

"Concerned?" He laughed, not with any sign of glee. "You're concerned for me? You're the one who's pregnant in a whole other time. What if you go into labor here and then when we finally go back, Bingley has to see his child there, and he missed everything?"

"I shall handle that to the best of my ability," Jane stated simply.

"To the best of your ability?"

"Yes, Zach."

"And what if it's years?"

"Zach, we've only been here for two months now," Kitty said.

"Exactly! And those two months can easily turn into two years, or four or six, or eight. What if you see Mr. Bingley again when your child is five years old? Do you think he will like that he missed the first few years of his child's life? Do you even think he will believe that's his child to begin with?"

"Enough!" Darcy exclaimed. "Zachary that is enough! You're offending her."

"Yes, because the truth offends everyone, doesn't it?" Zach spat.

"Thank you, Mr. Darcy," Jane said, "you are very kind, but I believe we should let him speak. Something tells me that he has things that he needs to say, and if he doesn't, then it will eat him alive."

Zach looked at her in wonder and slight alarm.

"Am I wrong, Zachary?" Jane asked simply. "Am I in error, sir? You are angry, and the more silent you are about it, the more you shall have all around you suffer due to it. So go on then, spit it out, man."

"I didn't mean to offend you, Jane," he apologized.

"Well, you did offend me, sir," she answered calmly. "And like you mentioned, I am pregnant now, and I feel my temper rising every moment due to the mood swings the situation calls for."

She touched her stomach. "I have a child on the way, and therefore the worst thing I can ever do is allow myself to get emotional or stressed, which would harm it. So, if you want me to walk around weeping, sir, then it shall not occur. And you offend Bingley for thinking that he shall not accept me if I return with a child in my arms. You offend my husband. Well, I tell you now, Bingley is stronger than you shall ever know. Now don't offend the child of my husband, please. And if you are upset, or contemplating something, then just tell us."

"Contemplating something?" Kitty asked, alarmed.

"Oh, Mr. Fitzwilliam wishes to visit Matlock, but is too afraid to ask," Jane answered, matter-of-factly, to which Zach flinched as if he had been slapped across the face. "What? I may do my best to always maintain a sweet disposition, but I can still detect when someone is in pain and be perceptive sometimes."

"Well, aren't you full of surprises?" Mary gave her a sneaky smile.

"Now you know why I always told mother to let you practice on the pianoforte even when it drove her insane. I knew that you loved to practice as an outlet to your frustrations and a means to help you establish your identity."

"You could tell that?"

"Of course, I could. I'm your older sister, for god sakes."

Jane turned back to Zach.

"Well, go on then."

"Is it really true?" I asked Zach. "Do you want to go to Matlock?"

At first, Zach did not respond, but then his shoulders relaxed. "Yes, I very much do."

Darcy studied him for a moment. "You're curious to see if it's the same?"

"It's my home, Fitz," Zach answered simply, "of course I want to go back. And I also wanted to know why my descendants gave it up."

"It's more complicated than that. I didn't live at Pemberly for the longest time."

"And why not?"

"Because it was a big house, and I felt so small within it."

This confession stirred the group and they looked at Darcy in wonder.

"Your time is different than mine," he continued, "and one man cannot feel content in so large a space. We're all about smallness now, because it helps us feel comfort, and also because we don't need that much. Your descendants shall perhaps be the same way. Also, a lot of us don't want a whole host of servants. We don't know how to maintain it. And if they are anything like me…"

"What? What do you mean like you?" Zachary asked.

"Well, when you are raised in a mansion, and then your parents die, the house feels like a mausoleum. It feels like there's deadness. And the best thing for you to do when you feel that is to run. I ran to London, and they perhaps did the same, or maybe even ran further."

"Is that what we are to you?" Zach asked. "We're your past, and we scare you?"

"Well, you don't scare us. But your ghosts do."

"Our ghosts?" Zach was clearly interested.

"Your shadows. The shadows that history casts can feel overwhelming to us. We wonder why we feel lonely when you are gone, and why we can't look after the house the way you all did, or why we don't get married as early as you. We wonder why it is so much harder to find love than you all did. We wonder why we are unhappy when you were not. We also wonder why we are loners nowadays. And we are content to be so."

He took a sip of coffee, and then continued. "Literally, family was very important to you back then. It's important now, but, well, many of us come from single parent households or we lose connection to our families very easily. We live in an era where mankind connects, but we also are disconnected."

"I suppose all this technology came with a price then, huh?" Zach asked. "You all can connect with anyone anywhere, but for some reason, you cannot always connect with the person next to you."

"A small price to pay for our lives getting larger, huh? That our personal lives also get smaller. For you live in a time where one's town is one's world."

Zach drummed his fingers along the table, and marveled at Darcy, not knowing what to make of him.

"You really are so young, aren't you?" he asked Darcy. "You look like my cousin, so I forget, but you really are young."

Darcy blinked. "Yes, I suppose that I am."

This new outlook did change our perspective on him in that moment. Yes, we were technically the same age, but also, we weren't. And for the first time, I had to deal with the reality that I was in love and over two hundred years older than the man I loved.

And now when I looked back on it all, when we had first met, I was the past coming up to him and chaining him down. How frightened he must have been of me!

"Today, let's call the house and book a tour," Kitty declared. "After all, we have the time. Besides, Mr. Darcy, your relatives also live there, so this should be comfortable."

And once more, my mind flashed toward Darcy, and a memory occurred to me.

"Yes, but is there a way you can do it on Thursday or Saturday?" Mary asked. "Those are my days off."

"Oh, no need to worry about that," Darcy said, "for we have to book it days in advance. So, we shall be able to wait for you."

"Good, for I would like to see it."

We all finished our meal, Mary went to work, and Georgiana went to her room, telling us that she was looking up job postings she could do as well. Mary had begun something indeed.

❧

The next moment that I could get Darcy alone, we were exiting to his car because he had to swing up to London to visit his office.

"Darcy, I have to ask you something."

"Sure, what is it?"

"I need you to tell me the truth about something you are avoiding."

"When have I ever withheld information?" he asked, worried.

"You have relatives at Matlock, and when I first fell through time, you mentioned a cousin of yours who you envied. Richard Fitzwilliam."

When I said this, Darcy froze.

"Fitz," I continued, "I'm going to assume that he is one of the descendants who was raised at Matlock. So, am I correct?"

Darcy bit his lip. "Yes, you are."

"And why would you not talk about that? Truly, all those times we visited Matlock in the past, and you met Colonel Fitzwilliam and…" I trailed off when I began to make the connection. "Oh."

"Yes."

"Fitz, were you angry that his ancestor had proposed to me?"

"That was part of it. I know that I shouldn't have been, but I was. Especially given the connection between both men."

"It would be a common name in that family though."

"Oh, it's more than that."

"How much more?"

Darcy leaned forward and whispered in my ear what he was feeling. When he finished, my eyes widened at this explanation and I gasped. "Really?"

"Yes."

"I can't believe it."

"Sorry, I was jealous for a time, but I now know that I have no reason to be. And there is only something else to worry about."

"Such as?"

"Kitty," he answered simply, and I saw the validity of his statement.

I sighed and rubbed my forehead. "Yes. Kitty."

❧

The Saturday came when we had booked a tour for Matlock, so Darcy drove us there by mid-afternoon. As we turned the bend around the set of trees to see the house, it appeared and for a second, it felt as if we had fallen back through time.

"My god, it looks the exact same from the outside," Kitty announced. "I feel as if any minute, the Colonel is going to emerge from it, and I shall see it. Blimey, I miss him terribly."

Darcy and I exchanged a look.

The vision however was soon marred as we noticed two cars parked in front of the house and thus the dream quickly came to an end, and four people emerged from it, being led down the steps by a servant of some kind.

"There must have been a tour before us," Darcy assumed.

"Well," Zach whispered, "at least I know the house is never forgotten. And that means a lot in its own sort of way."

We pulled up to the front of the house as the four of them pulled away and the servant was there to wait for us.

"Ah, you must be the Darcy party," the servant said.

"Yes, we are," Darcy confirmed.

"Well, welcome to Matlock. And for you, Mr. Darcy, it is good to see a Darcy return here. I am Derek Sutter, and I am the caretaker for the household."

"Oh, so you are going to be giving us the tour, then?" Zach asked.

"No, I am not actually, but you have a better one. A real treat there is today, because a week ago, one of the Fitzwilliam family came down, for he was told that the Queen and her family might want to visit the estate later on in the month, so he came down to be taught how to give a personal tour. He has been taking all the tours presently so that he can gain experience at it. I overlooked his previous ones and he has gotten quite good at it."

"One of the Fitzwilliam family?" Zach echoed as we entered.

"Yes, and he is the youngest of the late Mr. Samuel Fitzwilliam."

"Richard?" Darcy blurted out.

"Yes, you both know each other, I was told. He is looking forward to seeing you."

"Oh, I had no idea he was back here!"

"He is."

"Well, I am happy to see him."

I took Darcy's hand as we continued on.

"This family used to be all earls," Mr. Sutter explained, "but the title ended a few decades ago."

"Why?"

"One generation just didn't feel like maintaining the title. There's not much explanation given for why. Oh, here is Mr. Richard Fitzwilliam now."

We all turned to see a man coming down the steps. Our jaws dropped. Except Darcy's.

"Good afternoon," Richard said, "you must be the Darcy party. A pleasure it is to meet you all. And I see my cousin again."

"Richard!" Kitty cried.

There before us was Colonel Fitzwilliam.

৩৵৩

Or what we all thought was Colonel Fitzwilliam.

When Kitty cried out his name, the man named Richard Fitzwilliam turned to her and looked confused.

"Sorry?" he asked. "Have we met?"

"Richard, it's me!" Kitty cried, crestfallen. "Why are you pretending as if..."

Quickly did she realize that it was not the Colonel, but the tragically identical version of him, scattered across time and standing before her now. That had been what Darcy told me before when I had confronted him. He informed me that his cousin in his time looked exactly like Colonel

Fitzwilliam, but due to resentment, he had concealed it from me. Seeing this Richard before us, I could understand why. I quickly walked to Kitty, took her hand, and steadied her as she began to crack and crumble under the similarity and the weight of her disappointment.

"You must forgive our sister," I explained, "for we know someone who literally looks just like you."

"Really?" Richard said. "Me?"

"Yes," Georgiana said, her face thunderstruck. "Dear lord, it is quite bizarre."

"Indeed," Zach also acknowledged.

"Jeepers," Richard responded, smiling bashfully. "Well that is just… entertainingly creepy. The similarity must be really incredible for you to look on me as you all do now."

"It is, and it will just take a moment to get over it."

"I can testify, Richard," Darcy said warmly, "that he looks just like you."

"You knew about this?" Kitty gave Darcy a puzzled and unkind look. "And you never told me."

"Because I knew that you would like the surprise," Darcy answered, speaking a half-truth. "How have you been, Richard?"

"I have been well." He smiled warmly. "And you look like you have been doing splendidly, but I am not surprised. You always were lucky."

"And you always had more friends."

"Oh, go on." Richard smiled again, then his eyes turned to me. Darcy introduced him to me as well; Richard complimented me and told Darcy that I was a good find. Dear lord, he was charming too!

"Well," Richard said, turning to Kitty, "you called me Richard and then thought I was him. That means that…"

"You and he have the same first name as well," she voiced.

"Even more creepy, but amusing. Well, he looks as if he meant much to you."

"Yes… yes, he did."

"Did?"

"Forgive me," she said, unable to hide the emotion in her eyes, "he does."

Richard blinked, not knowing how to react to this, and just when the awkwardness grew to a deafening pitch, Zach offered his hand to shake.

"A pleasure to meet you," he said, shaking Richard's hand.

"Nice to make your acquaintance as well."

"And I forgot to introduce the rest," Darcy continued. "Yes, this is my fiancé, Elizabeth, and her sisters Jane, Mary, Kitty, along with my sister, Georgiana, and my cousin here, Zachary."

"People call me Zach," Zachary put in, his eyes not blinking as he looked on the replica of his little brother. What he and Kitty were feeling at present was beyond my levels of empathy. I could sense, but not determine.

"Amazing," Richard said. "I never knew you had a sister, Fitz. What gives?"

"She's my half-sister," Darcy lied.

"Oh, well then. It's a pleasure to meet you all," Richard complimented, still looking at Kitty from out of the corner of his eye. "And please be kind to me, for this is my third tour only and I am still afraid of missing something."

"We heard from your caretaker that you have been doing a very good job already," Kitty voiced, regaining her confidence. "I believe that you shall do well."

He smiled and winked at her. "Thank you. There, you see? You're comfortable around me now."

"Give me a little more time, and I am certain that I shall be up to scratch."

"Well, the tour takes a whole hour, so time is something we have."

"Not always," I whispered to Darcy, to which he chuckled, and then the tour commenced.

❦

If the purpose of this work was to define and explain in incredible detail the structure of a house that I had been in before, then I would be happy to oblige, but it is not so. All that could be said was that the main rooms were very similar to how they had been over two hundred years ago, and where there was a change, it was slight, but it was slight enough for Zach of course to notice the difference.

"Those curtains are different," he told me when we were in the music room. "And the fabric and upholstery is also changed here, but I suppose it would have gotten old with time."

"You can tell such differences?"

"I was the heir to Matlock; I knew the house down to its smallest detail."

"I never knew you took such pride in it."

"Yes, I suppose that I never showed it. Yet I did." He looked at our guide, Richard, as he was speaking with Kitty to the left of us as we turned into the portrait gallery. "He looks so much like my own little brother."

I followed his gaze. "Yes, he does."

"And yet, he doesn't know the pain he is putting Kitty through."

I looked at Kitty, who was attentive toward Richard and speaking to him with animation.

"She is getting on splendidly."

"No, I didn't mean now, but later on. When we leave. He is reminding her of Richard, and it will swell her heart, but when she leaves, she will be lonely again. You do not see it, Lizzy, because Kitty hides it from you. Yes, she is bearing this strongly. She is amazing, but I have seen her crying sometimes, when she thinks she is alone. She misses my brother, and this moment is kind, but it is also cruel. Why is the spitting image of my brother before me now?"

"Well, he is your descendant; therefore he could easily look just like one of you."

He gave me an uncomfortable smile. "It kind of makes me angry though, uncomfortable and my pride is stirred. Why does he not look like me? Bloody hell, the future is a little humbling."

I nudged his arm and chuckled. "Ah, shut up you."

As we walked on, Zach continued to look on Richard, while Kitty was the one who talked to him most. It was understandable, for she could not help herself. After all, this was the closest her mind determined that she would ever get to her fiancé who was centuries separated from her.

Luckily Richard had been raised to be the sort to have many manners, but was not raised so highly that he was a prat or prude, therefore rather than shirk away from Kitty due to the resemblance he had to someone in her life, he was agreeable and attentive, and amused. He seemed to find her charming, and that in itself alarmed me.

"Oh my god." I pressed a hand to my mouth.

"What?" Darcy asked me.

"Look at them."

Darcy followed my gaze and watched as Kitty looked up at the other Richard.

"All of these rooms and families had no more than a few children back in the day," Kitty said. "I always wondered about that, until I had one revelation."

"And what was that?" Richard asked.

"These people married for money and not for love. They had children to fulfill a contract rather than to fulfill their passions. Therefore, I learned long ago that if one was to be resolved to have a large family, then a requirement of it was to be poor. Or to not hate your spouse so much that at least you wanted to share the same bed with them. Unless they snored of course."

"I snore," Richard answered with a laugh.

"So do I... I think."

They both laughed together as they walked, and Darcy noticed something as well.

"We fell in love through different time periods," I said.

"Well, yes, but you were not spoken for."

"And you were."

"My wife cheated on me."

"But still..."

"And when you fell back into the past, you did not fall in love with my ancestor."

"True, but I felt connected to him."

"And it does always start that way, with a connection. But Kitty adores the Colonel."

"Yes, and she will remain loyal, for now. But if years go by and we stay here, she will wonder what it would be like to choose his descendant. Or perhaps I am worrying over nothing."

"I hope so. Let's just focus on the present."

Eventually we turned into another room and as we did so, we all froze as Richard spoke.

"This was one of the most popular parlors of the home during the Regency era," Richard explained, but we knew it all too well.

It was the exact same room that we had all been in before we had been pulled through time. It was the last room that Jane had seen Bingley, that Kitty saw the Colonel, that Zach saw Lydia and that Georgiana saw the rest of her family.

Their eyes immediately went to the place where they saw the person they loved last, and Zach even went to the spot that Lydia had last been. He reached out his arm to where she was, his mind rattled, and noticing this, Darcy distracted Richard so that he didn't notice how preoccupied everyone was but us.

"So, your caretaker mentioned that the Queen was coming to visit here?"

"Yes, she is hoping to visit a fancy home in Derbyshire, and she still has not chosen which one yet, but we have it upon good authority that Matlock is one of the top choices on her list."

"That must be a great honor for you," I said, and then Mary also joined in.

"So, the Queen of England really might come here?" she asked.

"Yes, she may. It has me a little nervous, but then I have met my share of royalty. It's always awkward if you ask me."

"So, the sovereign of all of England really is coming to Matlock?" Zach whispered, more to himself than to Richard, contemplating the magnitude of it. "But it makes me wonder," Zach said at last, turning back to his descendant. "From what we were told, the Fitzwilliam family no longer lives at Matlock. Would it not look better in the eyes of her majesty if you all were in residence?"

"We shall stay here if she comes," Richard said, "but between my brothers and me, none of us has any real incentive to live here."

"Why not, I wonder? Such a magnificent place it is."

"Yes, it is magnificent, but I cannot explain it. It just is…"

"Too magnificent?" Kitty suggested. "Too grand. Too large."

Richard smiled warmly. "Yeah, it is. And well, this was our parents' home, and the parents who begot them. What I mean is that it feels like a mausoleum. And a man can feel so small in the shadow of his ancestors who seem greater than how he shall ever be. The weight of the long gone can be antagonizing. It can make a man feel so alone sometimes. I suppose my brothers and I just couldn't take it."

Richard had gotten serious for a moment, contemplative, to the point where he seemed to fall inside of himself and forget that he was amongst us, and as he did so, it gave us time to look at Darcy, whose words had been the reflection of Richard's.

He knew it.

But Richard had not.

There both men stood, so separated and yet they both were so much connected. Both had suffered under the weight of the great estates they inherited and the men who came before them, and now we had heard that twice.

"Try looking at it in a different light," Zach said to Richard, his descendant. "This house is not meant for you to live in alone. Or feel alone. It's the house your family was raised in, so that you could always say that you belonged to them. As any family that I shall have will come from me."

"It's hard when it makes you feel inadequate," Richard said. "When I was young, my parents were always talking about the good ole days, and my brothers listened, and they always sounded so happy when they spoke, in ways that made us jealous. My parents got married when they were young. My brothers and I still don't know what to do with ourselves romantically."

He stopped, blushing. "Oh dear, I think I am oversharing. I don't know why I am like this with you all. Truly, this is not usually how I do tours."

"But it is how you really are," Darcy answered with a smile.

"Yeah, Fitz has heard me vent and whine before."

"Being in the presence of family begets discussions about family," Kitty offered. "We often overshare, even in the wrong location or time."

"Well," Zach said, "far be it from me to give you advice, but since you shared, I suppose that I have the right. Time is everyone's friend. Even memories. They soften the bad moments, the embarrassing moments, and the disappointing ones. Literally, they often turn stupid actions into lifelong lessons that had to be undergone. And so believe me when I say this: there is no such thing as the good ole' days.

"No matter what era, everyone is a disappointment to their parents. We let someone down, we got rejected, or we made mistakes that we paid for, for the rest of our lives. Or we lose much. Or we were stupid. And we all NEVER live up to the people who came before us. It's just the way things are. Only time helps us forgive ourselves, and sometimes not even then. When looking at your past, those aren't ghosts that you remember, nor are they shadows; they were humans. Humans just like you."

"Thank you," Richard replied. "No one ever explained it like that before."

I took Darcy's hand and winked at Zachary.

Before we left the room, Kitty had gravitated to the window and was looking out. I joined her there and held her by the shoulders.

"There," she pointed to the road. "That's where I was when I first saw the Colonel and I ran alongside his carriage. And four rooms down from here is where he got down on one knee and proposed to me. Then to be so much parted from him and then see his replica, the way I saw yours in London, well, I am happy that we came, for I am glad to see him."

She turned toward me. "But now I am remembering the Colonel, and this makes me even sadder. Why does his descendant look like him? Yes, I know, it is simply just the repeat of physical traits, but still, it feels like it is something more, and it hurts. It is so antagonizing."

"Kitty, I am sorry, and while I know that you were brought into the future with us for a reason, I don't know why yet. Yet something tells me that this particular outing was not for you."

"Then who was it for?"

Eventually our tour came to an end, and Richard walked us to our car, talking mostly with Kitty the entire time. As we did so, I noticed Zach looking up at the windows of Matlock, and I took that moment as a chance to walk up to him.

"How are you?"

"I cannot tell you now, Lizzy," he said, "but at least I'm no longer angry. And I will say this. I am happy that Matlock still lives. If it does, then that means, in some way, that we always will."

"Ah, the fear of being haunted by eternity."

"Yes."

I turned to Richard as he took Kitty's hand and shook it.

"While it may just be coincidence, I see why he looks like Colonel Fitzwilliam, and not you. And why you were brought here."

"Why do you think, then?"

"Because, even centuries later, your little brother will always need you."

Zach looked at Richard and marveled at the revelation.

"You really think you didn't help him at all, Zach?" I said. "I do believe that now he is able to face the Queen of England. And if it helps, Lydia would be proud of you now."

Zach nodded, his eyes filling with tears of pride.

"Well," Richard announced to us, sounding genuine, "I hope you enjoyed yourselves. Then again, what beats Pemberly, eh?"

"I don't know," Darcy said lightly, "your house would and could give me a run for my money."

Richard smiled, obviously pleased with the remark.

"Thank you, Richie, "Darcy said, "And have a good day."

"Fitz?" Richard asked.

"Yes?"

"What I don't know about our family tree is a lot, but I was once told that our families were related back for centuries, right?"

"Yes, they were," Zach answered for him.

"Small world, huh?" Richard laughed.

"Yes, small world."

"If you ever wish to visit," Richard offered, looking at Kitty, "then feel free to arrange a dinner or something, for my brothers will come soon, in case the Queen wishes to pop by."

We thanked him for his kind offer, then we entered our car and rode off, with Richard Fitzwilliam watching us as we disappeared down the lane.

Chapter Fourteen

ANOTHER PARADOX

The next day, as we all were sitting down prepared for dinner, there was one missing from the table.

"Where is Georgiana?"

"Oh," Mary said. "She didn't tell you?"

"Tell us what?"

We were interrupted by the ringing of a doorbell.

"Don't worry," Kitty said, "I'll get it."

"No, at this hour, I should." Zach left the table, went to the door and then quickly he came back to the dining room.

"Yeah, so we've got company," he said. "You remember that bloke from the bookstore? Tom Clarkson?"

We all nodded.

"Yeah, well, he's in the sitting room, with a flower in his hand, and he says that he has a date with Georgiana."

"What?" We all said at once, except for Mary, who covered her mouth to keep from laughing. "Yes, she clearly told no one."

We all entered the living room, and sure enough, there was Tom Clarkson, dressed in a shirt, flannel button down shirt over it and a tweed jacket over that and blue jeans. It was just enough to show that he was trying, but not enough to show that he was trying too hard. When we entered, he looked a little nervous.

"Ah, good evening."

"You came for a date with Georgiana?" Darcy said.

"Yes," Tom said, smiling bravely against Darcy's scowl. I therefore had to grab Darcy's hand, for I could see that he was intimidating the man.

"Perhaps one of us should get Georgiana."

"Don't worry, I'm coming down now," Georgiana's voice rang from the upper landing. "I just got finished with my hair."

Tom breathed a sigh of nervousness and then we all walked to the steps just as Georgiana was coming down them. She was wearing a lovely and simple light green dress which came down to her knees.

"Tom!" Georgiana smiled, blushing.

"You look beautiful!" Tom said, with the flower still in his hand.

"Is that for me?" she asked.

"Yes, it is." He handed her the flower and then she smelled it.

"It's lovely."

She then turned back to us and looked a little embarrassed.

"Family, you remember Tom."

"Yes, and what I do not remember is you telling us that you were going out on a date," Darcy commented.

"Oh, yes, about that. Well, I am not going to lie and say that it slipped my mind. I was just worried that I would tell you all and then the date would get canceled or I would get stood up. I've heard horror stories about that sort of stuff from others."

"You were worried that I would do that?" Tom asked, quite serious.

"Yes, I confess that I was."

"Oh, well, I am happy that I did not disappoint."

Darcy gave them both a look and then they stopped smiling.

"So, where are you taking her, Tom?" I asked.

"I thought that it would be fun if I took her to the movies and then to a pub that I fancy."

"You'll have her back here by 11 o'clock," Darcy stated, in a way that he could not be argued with.

"But if the movie goes over..." Georgiana hinted.

"Then you must call us to let us know," I said. "And do your best to cut the dinner short. And if you don't call by 11 to tell us, then we will call you."

Georgiana rolled her eyes.

"And don't roll your eyes," Darcy stated.

"Right, sorry. Yes, Tom will have me back here before 11 o'clock."

"Very good," Darcy said, "now off you go. The sooner you leave, the sooner you can get back."

"Yes, sir," Tom said, and then he took Georgiana's hand and they were off. We watched them through the window.

Darcy offered up a grunt. "He had better open the door for her. If he doesn't, then she should never go out with him again."

Zach laughed. "How quick we men are willing to tell women to cut us off. And really I wouldn't have it any other way."

Luckily Tom did open the door for her, she got inside and then he got into the driver's seat, and Georgiana waved to us as they drove away.

"He should die," Darcy stated bluntly.

"Darcy, I always admire your protectiveness," I said, "but that is going too far."

"Right. And yet, I cannot help it."

"I know that you can't. Don't worry, she shall be fine."

We all went back to dinner.

"And you knew about her date?" Zach asked Mary.

"Well yes," Mary replied. "I helped her pick out her dress."

"Why didn't you tell us?" Kitty asked.

"Because I thought that she had done so. Yet I can kind of understand. This one woman who I work with at the bookstore, Shelby, she got stood up by a bloke two weeks ago and she was humiliated. Really, there was no talking her out of her self-loathing. I sort of told Georgiana about it, and she didn't want to have to go through that."

"It's not that bad, really," Darcy pointed out. "I got stood up once, and I recovered quite quickly."

I nearly gasped. "You got stood up? Seriously?"

"Yes, I did."

"Who would stand you up?" Jane scoffed.

"Susan Doyle, when I was at university. I went to pick her up, and I got no reply. I found out later that she had got with her previous boyfriend that day, and she was out with him."

"Darcy, I'm sorry."

"See, we all have our sad stories."

Later that night, after dinner, we all had gone our separate ways and Darcy felt it was his duty to remain sentinel, waiting for the return of Georgiana. As such, I felt it my duty to remain with him, so we sat in one of the parlors and watched television during our wait.

Darcy had his cell phone beside him on the couch, and our feet were sprawled out on the coffee table, while we were continuing to binge watch the television show called 'Outsourced'.

"Are there any more episodes after these next ones?" I asked him.

"Sadly no, because this show didn't last more than one season."

"Blast it! I quite like it."

"Yeah, yeah it's very good."

The show then turned to a commercial.

"So," he said, "what do you make of this mess?"

"And by that, I'm assuming that you mean the mess of Georgiana going on a date."

"You know that this cannot end well."

"Perhaps not, but she has the right to try it. Come on, Darcy, you had all the chances in the world to date, and we haven't. Dating is important. Besides, after Wickham, she deserves this."

"I suppose so, but like I said before, her brother won't be too happy about this."

"Are you really thinking of her brother just now? Or are you thinking of yourself?"

Darcy flinched. "Good point."

I took his hand and kissed it.

Then the show came back on.

After the last episode, Darcy looked at his watch and it read that it was 10:30. And there was still no phone call.

"She still has a half an hour before we ought to get paranoid," I pointed out.

"I know, I know."

I looked around the room, and for some reason, I felt as if I was seeing it for the first time. And then all the memories of Pemberly flowed back into me as if I was seeing our past, both near and far past, flashing before my very eyes with an intense velocity.

"Remember when you first brought me to Pemberly?" I asked him.

"Of course I do," he said, rolling his head toward me.

"I had no idea that I would eventually cause you all this trouble."

"You didn't cause anything, Lizzy, it just happened. And even if you did, to be human is to always be in some sort of trouble. I think that I prefer to be in trouble with you rather than be anywhere without you."

His words warmed me. "Thank you for that."

"You are welcome."

"At the time you brought me here," I continued, "though you were attached, I looked on that moment as our real first date."

"A part of me did as well. All those days spent trying to quiet that voice within me and it was correct all along."

"Yes, it was. Who would have thought, huh?" I laughed, touching my head to his.

"Indeed, who would have thought?"

"And then when we danced at Pemberly in the ballroom, well, my first ballroom dance here."

Darcy did not respond at first, and I just simply thought that he was contemplating something. Next, he stood up and faced me, his hands outstretched. I smiled, taking his meaning, so I placed my hands in his and we began to slow dance.

"Your ancestor was not the greatest fan of dancing."

"Well," he answered, his words in my ear, "at least I am better than he in that regard."

"You are delightful. Is it strange," I said as he twirled me around, "that even after all that we went through, this all feels new?"

"As if we have only just begun."

"Precisely. I know that we are still in the beginning of the relationship, but still it feels as if it will never get old."

"That's love for you, I guess, rather than the idea of it. I suppose I never loved Caroline, just the idea of her."

"Well, not your fault. There really was not much to love there," I said wryly.

"No, there was not. I swear, to be a man is to spend most of one's life having very bad taste."

"Oh, we women do the same thing."

"Yes, so much of our lives are spent falling around and stumbling. So much time is wasted."

"Or perhaps it's meant to be that way. If you spend time stumbling, it feels even better when you get it straight."

"I suppose," he answered, giving me another twirl.

"Maybe I should be thanking Caroline."

"Why?"

"If she had not messed up so terribly, then I never would have gotten you."

He pulled me closer. "Oh, now isn't that a unique thought?" He grinned as he looked down on me, and then we kissed. Over and over we continued to dance, kissing each other in the process and we grew so occupied in each other that we didn't even notice that Georgiana had returned, and that she was standing in the doorway, watching us.

"Please." Georgiana raised her arms and chuckled. "Don't stop on my account."

We both looked down at our feet, embarrassed.

"Waiting up for me?" she asked.

"Yes, in fact," Darcy acknowledged. "We were."

"I am not late."

"No, you are not, but we still were worried," I noted.

"And I appreciate that."

"Wait." I took a good look at her. "You look very happy, and you are being very nice again. That must mean that the date went well."

"It went splendidly!" Georgiana laughed, bouncing into the room. "We went to the movie first, which was great, because it gave us something to talk about when we ate. Then we went to the best pub! It was bloody brilliant, and it even had this thing where it dipped a whole onion into the fryer and fried the whole thing."

"Oh yes, I've had that many times," Darcy said. "Isn't it awesome?"

"Yes, it does fill me with awe."

I chuckled.

"He didn't try and kiss you, did he?" I asked.

"And if he did, you didn't let him, did you?" Darcy questioned.

"Of course he didn't!" She scoffed. "Why would he? Wait, you can kiss someone on a date?"

Darcy and I looked at each other.

He cleared his throat. "Well, not really."

"Then why did you speak as if it was fine? Is it really something that happens?"

"Well, it has been known to occur," I admitted.

"So, I will kiss him eventually?" Her eyes were bright with anticipation.

"Well, you have to make it to the second date first."

"He said he would call me."

Darcy and I exchanged looks again.

"And, um…what were his exact words?" Darcy asked.

"He said that he would call me sometime."

"Darcy?" I asked, turning to him "What precisely does that fully mean in man-language?"

"Usually it means that he will never call you again."

"What?" Georgiana asked, crestfallen.

"When we often say, 'we'll call you sometime', we don't always mean it."

"But he said he would!" Georgiana exclaimed. "So he will." She looked so disappointed that we didn't know what to do. It was a problem, a difficult and real problem. Nothing was worse than the phrase, 'I'll call you sometime', because it was so ambiguous, so undesirable a thing to hear, because it left one wondering if it would be true or not.

How many women had I met who admitted to exploding at a man who never called her when he said he would? It was many. It was the natural inclination of the male sex to say that when he did not wish to tell the truth, and it was the great thing that awoke a secret dragon that lurked inside us females. It led to the causing of public scenes, angry shouts, throwing things, and occasionally the desire to burn the man's house down. Too often men would never know the full amount of disdainful feelings that we women harbored within us when they did not call, and we were left wondering if this would be one of those moments.

"We don't know that yet," I said. "Georgiana, he may most likely call."

"But what could I have said that he would not want to call me? I thought we had such a good time."

"I think you made her paranoid," I whispered to Darcy.

"Better sooner than later."

"Georgiana, just think about the date now," I rushed out, "and that you had fun. And don't think of him calling now or not."

"But I do care about it."

"Oh, good job, Darcy!" I scolded.

"You're welcome," he said, sitting down.

"Georgiana," I said, "the little I know about love and romance, it's best to be fine if he calls or if he doesn't. Men for some reason like it if a girl appears as if she doesn't care."

"That's butt backwards," she determined, and we both looked at her.

"Butt backwards?"

"Yes, it's a term that Tom taught me on our date. It means—"

"Oh, we know what it means," Darcy said.

"Right." She ducked her head.

"Yes, but I promise you," I advised, "that he most likely shall call, and if he does, then be happy about it, but if he doesn't call, then don't let it get to you. The worst thing you can do is let it get to you."

"Oh and also don't call him either," Darcy magnified.

"I never understood that, by the way," I admitted, turning to him. "What is the system to calling a man? Should the woman never call the man and he should only call her, or should it be a mixture?"

"The mixture should be that he calls you at first, and then after a couple of dates, it begins to alternate. The first couple of times, he ought to call you, and then you both can call back and forth, but if he only ever says call him, then don't do it. And *he said* that he would call you."

"Yes, he did," Georgiana repeated. "But he and I really did have fun. But if he doesn't call, then what do I do?"

"You just act calm and forget about him."

She frowned and plopped down on the sofa. "Oh, well that is very depressing."

This all would have been quite comical, if it were not for the fact that such discussions really were important to us women, and they hurt to consider. When a man does not call, for some reason, it really does feel as if it stabs one, and when we realize that he does such because we are not that important to him, then it becomes incredibly painful.

"But tell us all that you spoke about," I demanded, in hopes of distracting her, because she was about to fall into a significant gloom.

This luckily pulled her out of her paranoia and therefore she was able to remember the really good moments of the date. She was happy that they had mostly spoken of things such as their favorite shows on the BBC, as well as things they liked, because Georgiana had not thought of anything else when it came to her past. She would have to tell him about where she went to school, what she was thinking of majoring in, or if she was going to go to university one day.

"He was really honored that he was my very first date ever," she said proudly. "Yes, he liked it a lot."

"Well, that is very good," I said, when she finished her narration. "And we are happy that you had a good time."

"Now it follows that I really ought to get a job, like Mary," Georgiana said. "It will give me more things to talk about with him if he does call, and I hope he does, and I will also become more independent."

She jumped up and then decided to go to bed.

"And thank you again for waiting up for me, so now you can all go back to your dancing."

She laughed as she went up the steps and disappeared along the landing.

"Well, she looks happy," I intoned, "except for all the things that we said to upset her."

"It had to be said."

"I have a question though."

"What?"

"Why do men tell us that they shall call us sometime when they have no intention of ever doing so?"

"I suppose that it is our way of letting a woman down gently."

"But it doesn't resolve anything, because we really do expect you to call us when you say that. Besides, how is it different than what you say when you do actually want to go out again? If you like us, you say that you shall call us sometime. And then when you don't like us, you still say that you shall call us sometime."

"I know, it's very unclear." He turned to me. "But think about it. What if we really did say at the end of a date that we were not really into you? It would devastate you and be awkward for us."

"I know, but we eventually feel devastated anyway."

"Yes, but you feel it away from us."

"Also why do some men say they will call a woman, then not call her, even when he knows, due to working together, he will see her again?"

"Oh, that's when it gets stupid. That's when he's an imbecile. And the woman has every right to be mad. That being said, in all other circumstances, when we say that, I suppose that it's our way of dealing with it, without dealing with it."

At my puzzled expression, he continued. "I know, it doesn't give the woman any resolution, but the way that we see it, you won't get any resolution either way, whether we tell you the truth or not. Either way, you will still feel hurt. So we just figure that the best way is to let you undergo it through silence and distance."

"Either way it really bites. But I see what you mean. When to not communicate is as bad as communicating, and when communicating is as bad as not communicating. Only where love is involved would this conundrum exist."

"Precisely. Glad we skipped the whole dating part altogether, aren't you?" He smiled.

"Yes, I very much am."

"Yes, even back in 1812, it wasn't really dating between us, was it?"

We were interrupted when Darcy's cell phone rang.

"Who would be calling at this hour?"

He looked at the phone as I walked away and began to tidy up where we were, closing the bag of biscuits and getting our empty cups.

And then I kept hearing the phone ring and turned to see Darcy just looking at the phone.

"Darcy, what is it?"

"It's her."

"Her who?"

"It's your descendant. Elizabeth Darcy."

His eyes were frozen, and he looked as if he was a man who knew not what to do and how to go about it.

"Darcy, pick up the phone."

"What if she wants me to come back to London?" he whispered shakily. "What if she wants me to pretend that I'm her children's father? I cannot do that, Elizabeth, I cannot. I was happy in pretending like I had forgotten all about her here."

"Don't worry," I assured him, taking the phone and answering it for him. "Hello, Mrs. Darcy?"

I heard heavy breathing on the other side.

"Elizabeth?" Mrs. Darcy said, with even my same voice, "Is that you?"

"Yes, it is Lizzy."

"How are you?" she rushed out. "I expected to get Mr. Darcy, but you're fine too."

"Oh, good, is there a problem? Because you are calling late."

"And I am pretty certain that you will not care."

My curiosity was piqued. "Why not?"

"Because you are about to be really happy. It's precisely what you would want, I—"

The phone call was disconnected immediately, and I looked at the phone.

"I don't know if she hung up on me," I explained, for his phone had enough bars on it, "but we got cut off."

"For the longer that is, then the better perhaps."

"Not likely. She said that she had some good news. She said something would make us happy."

"Well, it can't be work-related, because I've been already doing fine on that score."

"Yes, you have. So, what could it be, I wonder? Do you mind if I call her back?"

"Do we really have to? It creeps me out how much you both look alike."

"I know, I know, but still. Darcy, she really did seem happy."

"Oh, fine."

I opened his phone again, but I did not get the chance to call back, because his phone rung once more and it was Elizabeth Darcy again.

"Mrs. Darcy?" I said, picking it up. "Sorry, I don't know what happened."

"Oh, it was not you, my phone died, so I had to place it in the charger."

"Oh, well you said you had good news."

"Yes, I do. Mrs. Darcy, he is back."

"Who is back?"

"Mr. Darcy!" she cried. "My husband is back."

"He's back?" I gasped.

"Yes, yes he is."

"Oh, that is wonderful. Hang on just a moment."

I pulled the receiver away from my lips and turned to Darcy.

"It's your ancestor, Darcy. He's returned."

"He's here?"

"Yes, he is."

Darcy did not look relieved however, but he slowly collapsed on the sofa, and I sat next to him.

"Mrs. Darcy, just hang on for another minute," I said, and then I put the phone to my leg. "Darcy, are you all right?"

He looked straight ahead, his gaze focused on something I couldn't see. "He's here. He's actually in the same time period as I am."

"Yes, he is."

"Funny thing it is. I knew that he would come one day and that I would face him. But knowing something will happen doesn't always prepare you for when it does. And now that it comes down to it, I don't know how to face him."

I placed my hand on his thigh, comforting him, and then I raised the phone back to my lips.

"Mrs. Darcy, I am happy that he is returned, but I wonder if the best thing right now is for us not to come. He may not wish to see us. And both he and his descendant might antagonize each other. I don't want either of them to get hurt."

"No," she stated. "You all need to come immediately. Come tomorrow. Elizabeth, he did not come alone."

Chapter Fifteen

DARCY MEETS DARCY

We woke everyone up and told them the news. While they wished to travel throughout the night, they all knew that it could not be done.

Mary texted Tom and told him that she had to call out the next day due to a family emergency, and the next morning, we did not eat breakfast, but rather picked up food along the road as we hastened to London.

After hours of driving, we reached Mayfair, pulled down the familiar street that had Darcy's townhouse, and emerged immediately.

Kitty however, the most eager of us all, went forward first because we needed to be careful. When allowed to enter, we couldn't afford the children to see Darcy and me, so she took the lead. She knocked on the door and did not have long to wait, as very soon, my familiar face opened it and I was looking at Elizabeth Darcy, the woman who looked exactly like me—who wasn't me.

"Don't worry," she said, "my children are with their nanny and visiting my parents, so you can all come in."

"Oh good." Jane and Kitty moved past her with all speed, but Elizabeth did not look offended at all. In fact, she only looked amused, even when she saw me.

"Well," I said, "you look very happy."

She sighed and clasped her hands over her heart. "I am. He came back. He came back!"

I placed my hand on her shoulder.

"Would you mind it if I saw him?" I asked. "For I have a lot of explaining to do."

"I suppose you do owe him that much and I cannot get in the way of that. I will not be jealous."

I gave her a warm smile. "Thank you." I turned to Darcy. "And don't you dare be jealous either."

"I cannot help it," he droned, sounding like a little boy.

"You know that I never liked him in that way."

Following Georgiana, Zach and Mary as well, Darcy and I entered with trepidation, and then we followed Elizabeth just as we turned into the main room and saw everyone there.

"Charles!" Jane cried.

"Richard!" Kitty bellowed.

"Jane!" Mr. Bingley roared as he embraced her.

"Kitty!" Colonel Fitzwilliam exclaimed, hugging Kitty as well as lifting her up and twirling her around. "My god, I had no idea what had happened to the lot of you!"

"I missed you terribly!" she cried. "Dear god, I did."

"Mrs. Darcy told us that you have been here for months," Mr. Bingley informed us, and then he looked down at Jane's belly.

"You...you are with child?" His voice was almost a spiritual sound.

"Yes, well, you see the proof in it," Jane noted, her eyes shining with happiness.

He had the look of one who had been struck by Cupid's bow. "I'm going to be a father!"

We all chuckled at him, for he was so very much Mr. Bingley at that moment.

"Yes, we had hoped that you didn't endure too long of a time in the past," Jane answered, her eyes fixed on her husband.

"No," Colonel Fitzwilliam said. "When we came here, you had all only disappeared an hour before. You've been here for months!"

"We knew we would see you again," Kitty said, her eyes fixed on the colonel.

"I know, but—" Colonel Fitzwilliam was cut off as he beheld his brother, "Zachary!"

"Richard!"

Both brothers embraced as we heard another shout from the other side of the room.

"Where's Lydia?" Zach cried, "where is—"

"I'm here!" Lydia cried, rushing into the room. "Sorry I was just in the bathroom, for I had never seen anything like it before. Zachary!"

"My Lydia!" Zach cried, kissing her passionately. "My beautiful Lydia."

"My heart dropped into my stomach when I saw you disappear!" Lydia said, her voice quivering. "Don't ever do that to me again."

He gave her a loving and passionate smile. "I shall endeavor not to."

"Oh, my son is well, thank the lord for that!" Lady Fitzwilliam cried.

"Yes, he is!" Earl Fitzwilliam also exclaimed, and we were surprised to see them as well, coming around the corner, "and so are your daughters, Mr. and Mrs. Bennet!"

"What?" I gasped, then from around them appeared our mother and father.

"Lizzy, Jane, Kitty and Mary!"

The familiar voice of our mother burst through the air, and I could not believe it. There, entering from another room, emerged my mother and father. Like the rest, their period clothing clashed against the modern surroundings that they found themselves in. They all had come! They all had come!

"Until I saw you all, I could not believe it!" our mother cried as she folded her arms around us. "Indeed, I could not believe it at all!"

"And I'm still speechless myself," our father said. "There are two of you. There are two of my Lizzys."

We all cried tears of joy and embraced them.

I wiped happy tears from my cheeks. "I cannot believe it. My parents are now brought into the future."

"Yes, but shame on you, Lizzy," our mother cried. "Truly shame on you. You didn't tell us that you had fallen into the future before. What a dirty deception."

"My dear, would we really have believed her?" our father asked her.

"Precisely," I replied. "Mama, you of all people had better see yourself for what you are this instant and admit that if I had come back home telling you all that I had come back from the year 2016, you all would have died of fright and then had me admitted to some asylum and called yourselves proper for doing it."

"Oh well," she snapped, "I suppose it had to be done that way if you put it like that. But it is all so fantastic, that I am getting nervous already."

"Oh, poor Mama." Kitty sighed, still holding onto Colonel Fitzwilliam.

"Now you are being brought into a time where such things as nervous complaint have no sway on anything."

"Oh, I am sure there is some phrase for what I have."

"Sadly, there is a term for everything nowadays," Elizabeth, my doppelganger said, and our mother looked between us both.

"I feel as if I could be knocked down with a feather now."

"As could I," our father admitted.

"Mother, Father, Earl and Lady Fitzwilliam, and Lydia and Colonel," Jane said, "we shall explain everything."

"You do not need to," came a voice from a corner that was all too familiar. We all turned around and from out of a seat stood Mr. Darcy—Mr. Fitzwilliam Darcy, the real master of Pemberly in 1812—the one who proposed to me before his descendant did, stood up. "My Lizzy and I explained it all to them in detail last night and this morning."

⚜

There he was, Mr. Fitzwilliam Darcy of Pemberly, standing there before us.

One half to this great mystery.

As he looked over all of us, his eyes fell upon me.

"Mr. Darcy," I said, curtsying to him, force of habit. "Hello, sir. I am glad to see you."

"Elizabeth," he said, "it's been many years."

I flinched. "I am sorry, sir, but it has only been a matter of months for me."

"I was told of such," he replied simply, and we only looked at each other, marveling at the other.

"I am sorry if you underwent any sort of pain," I offered my condolences. "I know that what you underwent must not have been easy."

Mr. Darcy looked away from me and cast his eyes on his wife.

"It hurt for a time, but it was well worth it."

"I can see that it was." I did not forget who was behind me, and so I shifted his attention. "As I have grown acquainted with your wife, sir, it is your turn to become acquainted with someone else who is very much connected with you. This is your descendant, and my fiancé, Mr. Fitzwilliam Darcy—of this time."

He followed my gaze, and his attention shifted to his double identity, which was standing in a corner, quite unnoticed.

"Upon my word, it is true," Lady Fitzwilliam said, coming forward and looking between her real nephew and the one who she thought he was. "There are two Mr. Darcys."

"As there are two Elizabeths," my Mr. Darcy said. "Good afternoon, Mr. Darcy."

Elizabeth and I turned to her husband and he swallowed heavily, took a step forward and looked at the man who also appeared to be him.

"Good day," he replied, breathless. "We look…"

"Yes. Yes, I know."

"We are the spitting image of each other."

"I suppose I got my physical traits from you."

Both men looked at me, and then looked at the other Elizabeth.

"And we have chosen as the other would have," Elizabeth's husband said.

"Yes, we have," my Mr. Darcy noted.

"The coincidence is lost on neither of us. And I'm assuming that you have spent many a moment wondering what this all means."

"Yes."

"And how have you got on? What is your success?"

"I haven't been able to determine anything."

"Neither have I. Then we are both even more the same. For we both are victims to ignorance."

"Sir, I am your descendant. Forgive me, but is this really all that you have to say to me?"

I was proud of my Darcy in that moment, for indeed, I could see his point. I knew very well that there was no ideal way to handle this, but Elizabeth's husband was handling this in the way that I recalled him handling many things. He was so cold, so severe about things, when his true feelings always were hidden underneath it all. And it was sometimes hard to get at the real him.

When one did unearth the man beneath, it was exquisite, for he was like a dark diamond that shined. Yet it was not always apparent, and such coldness could antagonize a person. Very quickly it had done so with his descendant, who I knew was wishing for some sort of warmer reception, a smile here, or a kind word there. And somehow, it made me love him all the more.

"Mr. Darcy," I said.

"Yes?" both men replied, looking toward me. I rolled my eyes in frustration.

"The Mr. Darcy from 1812."

"Oh, yes?"

"Sir, I know you have been through a lot, but your descendant does not know your character as we do. Yes, you have endured much, but so has he."

"I can very well believe that," Mr. Darcy said. "I returned to my time, being yanked away from my children and the love of my life to the drawing room of Matlock and was met by the sight of my Aunt Lady Catherine de Bourgh, who had apparently come to force me to marry Anne. So, I can imagine what you had undergone," he directed this last sentence to my Darcy.

"Yes, I have."

"You both have," I confirmed. "Therefore Mr. Darcy, Elizabeth's husband, your descendant is looking for acceptance. Something that you owe him, therefore, please, show him some affection."

"I do not mean to appear as this," the other Mr. Darcy said. "Elizabeth, you know that I don't. It is just such a shock to me. I've been out of my own time and place for five years, settled here just as I got pulled back into my home, find my sister to be missing, worried that I was parted from the family I made forever, and then pulled back—and now I am looking at myself when I look at you, sir," he directed this again to my Mr. Darcy, "and I don't know what to make of this."

"I can understand that, for I didn't for a time. I just ask for one thing."

"What would that be?"

"Look happy to see me, sir, for I did everything to look after what belonged to you."

"You are referring to Pemberly, I assume."

"And to your sister."

"Where is my sister?" Darcy started, "where is she?"

"I am here, brother," Georgiana whispered, and indeed she had been there the whole time, just watching both men talk. Confusion was etched into her features. Now she would get what she asked for; she got her brother back, and yet, as she looked at my Mr. Darcy, I saw a mind torn, and I knew why.

In that moment it perhaps then did occur to her that she did in fact view my fiancé as her real brother. And now that both of them were present and there was hardly any difference in between both men, she could not tell which one to feel emotion for the most.

"Georgiana," the other Mr. Darcy gasped, hoarse with emotion as he stood up and beheld his sister. "I cannot believe it. It's been years since I saw your face."

"And I had no idea that I did not see you for all those months. They had to conceal it from me so not to frighten me."

"Yes, you pretended to be me?" the other Mr. Darcy asked mine.

"He had no choice," I defended him. "There was no other way."

"Fitzwilliam," Georgiana said, "he did the best he could, and he did it quite well."

Half-crying, she rushed up to him and they hugged.

"I never thought I would see you again," Darcy said with a sigh, breathing into her hair.

"Well, apparently Time had other plans." Georgiana laughed, kissing his cheek. "I am glad that you are returned to me again, Fitz. So much happened since we saw each other. You have a family I didn't know about or meet."

"Yes, I do!"

"And would you believe it? I stood up to Mr. Wickham too."

"What?" He appeared angry.

"Don't worry, it was brilliant. I frightened him and everything."

"When did you get in contact with that libertine?"

"Oh, it was my fault," Lydia said. "I sort of eloped to get married to Mr. Wickham, and it was Georgiana who found us and helped me see him for what he was."

"Yes, I did that," Georgiana said proudly, "I did that. And you got married." She returned her gaze to her brother.

"I did."

"Your children are beautiful. I have not gotten the chance to really meet them because we couldn't, but I would like to know them."

"I am happy that you will, for they would love you."

He took Georgiana's hand and presented her to his wife.

"I know that you both have already met, but this gives me the chance that I never had before," he voiced. "Georgiana, this is my wife, Elizabeth, and Elizabeth, this is my sister, Georgiana. You both are sisters now."

"When we did meet, it was in a rather rushed way, so this works well enough." Elizabeth smiled warmly at her new sister-in-law. "It is nice to make your full acquaintance, Georgiana."

"It is also a pleasure to meet you as well," Georgiana said. "I can see that you make my brother very happy."

"She does." The other Mr. Darcy smiled at his wife. "She does very much."

He raised her hand to his lips and kissed it. Then, in a burst of emotion, he pulled her to him and kissed her passionately. We all looked away to allow them privacy. Eventually he pulled away from her. "Forgive me," he apologized to the rest of us.

"It is fine, Darcy," Zach said. "In truth, it's just nice to see that you have some spark in you, mate."

We all laughed at that.

Over time, we sat down and began to talk about all that happened. As we did so, every now and again, I could not help but steal a glance at the other Mr. Darcy. He had spent five years in the future, and I wondered about every moment of it. There were so many questions, and it all made me so curious. Every now and again, he caught my eye and we both exchanged a glance before looking away. I thought it had gone unnoticed, but I felt air on my cheek as my Mr. Darcy was leaning into me.

"Why do you look on him so much?"

"Don't worry," I assured him. "It is not romantic in any way. I am just curious as to what he has undergone. There is so much history between us and I feel that it must be resolved somehow."

"And let me guess. You will not be satisfied until you speak to him about it."

I looked at Darcy and refused to be upset. Too oft it is that people view overprotectiveness as being harmful possessiveness, but they are not one and the same. There's an awful lot of the latter, but when it comes to love, there's infinity of the first one. And infinity is never unwanted or too much when real affection is the order of the day.

"Do you trust me, my love?" I asked my Darcy simply.

"Yes, I do."

I kissed his cheek. "Then trust me. Let me speak to him."

"I will," he replied simply. "But before I go, now I understand what you went through."

"What do you mean?"

"When you met your identical counterpart, when you met his wife. You both ought to feel a connection, for you are so much similar, and so much physically the same, but there never can be, can you?"

"No, there can't," I said, looking at her as she spoke with Jane and Mr. Bingley. "We could do our best, but I feel as if there will always be a wall between us, because we are too close, and therefore we have no choice but to be so very far away. Oh dear, I am certain that I am not making any sense."

"You are though. I feel now that I see him. We can never be fully comfortable around each other, because we are too much alike. Even down to the women we chose. We both chose you two. And we both chose you yourself. I just happened to be the one you chose, because I happened to be the first one you met, and I was the first one you saved. And we both know that. I can see it in his eyes. He knows it just like I do. How can I be comfortable around a man who almost had my fate, and the only thing that got in his way was Time itself?"

"Then I suppose that Time is our friend."

"Yes, I suppose that it is. And I do trust you."

"Thank you."

I squeezed his hand once more before I got up, walked over to the other Mr. Darcy when he was alone for a moment, and faced him.

"You came to me at last," the other Mr. Darcy said as I sat down.

"Why do I get the sense that you knew I was going to come over to you eventually?" I smiled archly.

"Because, despite all these years apart, I shall always know you."

"Darcy, I am so sorry for what happened to you. It must have been so hard."

"No, don't apologize." He swiped the air with his hand, dismissively. "There is no more room for apologies now. I used to scream at Time very often for what it did to me, looking for someone to apologize, and then I realized something."

"What?"

"That spending all that time wishing for someone to apologize, it kept me from seeing that no apology was needed really, because I was given her."

He looked to his wife as she was speaking with Jane.

"All those days that Time had given me the ideal version of you; unattached, sharing similar experiences with me, and stronger than me. She really is."

"You both make each other stronger. When we appeared here and you were separated from her, she looked like a wounded animal. She was lost."

"Was she?"

"Yes, and now she is so happy. You must be a great husband."

"I spent such a long time trying to get back in time to see you," he continued, "and I didn't understand how I didn't notice her before. I was foolish. And now you are engaged to my descendant."

"I am."

"I am under the impression that you perhaps fancied him long before you even met me."

"Yes. I was in love with him before I was yanked back through time and back into 1812."

"So, when you met me, you were..."

"Yes. I was. Even then."

"Then you had never loved me."

"It was not that."

"Then what was it?"

"I was loyal to him, and it would take me long to get over it. And you looked just like him; it made me angry for a time. Remember how you didn't notice your wife for a long time just because you were remembering me? Well, you and I are both the same now, because I could not fully see you, because I was remembering him."

"That was perhaps why you turned to the Colonel, wasn't it?" he asked.

"That was the moment when I was beginning to get over your descendant and accept the reality that I was parted from him forever."

He shook his head and chuckled. "We are the same. My, my. Isn't it ironic?"

"Not so much, for I have noticed a similarity of the turn of our minds before. We are both very stubborn, you see, and sometimes we can be a little blind."

"Yes, we can." He smiled warmly at me and I returned it.

"If we had never been meant for others," I offered him, "yes, we would have been ideal for each other."

"Yes, we perhaps would have been," he replied, "very much so. But they are better for us, aren't they?"

"Yes, they are, in every way."

"She saved me," he said, gesturing to his Elizabeth. "Almost in the same way that you did. You both saved me."

"And he hit me with his car," I said with a laugh, "and you refused to dance with me at first."

Darcy laughed in return.

"And you saved us both as well," I replied.

"How did we do that?"

"You chose us. The world is full of those who do not choose the right partner. It seems to be a custom, generally exercised, to not fall in love with the person who deserves it the most. You both are exceptions to that rule."

"Yes, we are. And that is a comforting thought."

"Yes, it is."

I offered my hand, and he shook it.

We directed our attention to Mr. Bingley, who remained close to Jane, but he turned to my Mr. Darcy.

"I cannot deny that I was worried when you all disappeared. And to find that you were all here for months, Fitz, I cannot pretend that Jane would have been fine without you and Zach watching over her. Thank you."

"Of course, mate," my Mr. Darcy said.

"I confess, it is hard for me to look at you a bit now, knowing that you are not who I thought you were. Amazing that there should be two of you, and you and he are so much alike. You really were strong to come back and be forced to be someone that you weren't. I hope I helped."

"Don't worry, you did, and I never forgot it."

Charles turned back to Jane.

"So, my love, it's nice to see how this world has been good to you, for you look healthy and well-fed." Bingley looked at Jane's belly when he said it. "You've been taking good care of my wife while I was separated from her, Fitz."

Jane laughed. "Charles, really?"

"What?"

"I'm pregnant, remember?"

Charles blinked. "Yes, of course, but…"

"Surely I look very different than how I did when I left you. After all, my size…"

Even yet, the reality had not settled in. "But you must remember, I only saw you no more than two days ago."

"And it was months for me."

"Yes, and so my mind is not accustomed to… you being pregnant, even though you have stated it over and over."

"Yes, she is, you dolt!" Zach laughed. "Good god man, it's obvious."

We all laughed at Bingley's flushed expression.

"So, you spent all these months away from me, pregnant. My dear, you must have been so scared, and I could not be here for you."

"Well," she said, putting her arm through his, "you are here now, and I knew that you would come. Besides, I had my family here, so I was brave enough for it. I just worried that I would give birth before I saw you again."

"Oh, that would have been grievous. Indeed, it would have been. But I'm here now. I'm here." He pulled Jane to him.

"Yes, you are. And Mr. Darcy has been very active. He has put me under his healthcare plan, so I get monthly check-ups at hospitals. I swear the advancements in medicine and Medicare is most delightful. They have equipment where they can see into my belly and I can see how the baby is looking."

"What?" Mr. Bingley gasped. "Impossible."

"And as you can see, impossible things are happening every day."

The other Mr. Darcy laughed quietly at this.

"What is it?" I asked him.

"Oh, Jane doesn't know, does she? She just quoted a movie."

"What movie?"

"She just quoted a live-action version of *Cinderella*."

"Really?" I chuckled.

"Yes, we show it to our children sometimes."

"*Cinderella*. Well, in her case, that can be a little fitting."

"Oh, and when Jane says that I put her on my medical plan," my Mr. Darcy said, turning to his ancestor, "I really mean that I put her on your medical plan, and I signed our name."

"Had a feeling," the other Mr. Darcy stated, nonchalant.

"And very soon, we shall be able to discover if it's a girl or a boy," Jane furthered.

"What do you mean?" Lydia asked.

"Oh, with the technology," Mary explained, "now they can tell if you are going to have a daughter or a son months before you give birth."

"Oh, that is just nonsense," our mother said. "I would say that's impossible, but then again, what is impossible anymore?"

"Indeed."

Our mother thought a moment, and then added, "Come to think of it, I wish that we had such technology when I was pregnant with all five of you."

"What good would that have done, my dear?" our father asked lightly, sarcastic. "By the time Mary came out, I knew what gender Lydia and Kitty were going to be long before we had them."

"Oh, stop pretending to be all-knowing, my dear," she retaliated, swatting him lightly on the shoulder.

"It's not all knowing, it's just experience. I've gotten to that point in life where I learned that 9 times out of 10, if the first three children come out one gender, then the rest will be the same."

"Then why did you never stop trying?"

Father raised an eyebrow. "My dear, are we really going to talk about this now? Seriously, we have travelled through time, and you are still talking about this? It's nice to know that even a super-impossible phenomenon will never change your personality."

We all laughed once more, even our mother joined in.

"I always will find you two so amusing," my Mr. Darcy said to my parents.

"And that is where you two differ," I whispered to the other Mr. Darcy.

"Actually, being in 21st century London has quite changed my perspective," he whispered in reply. "And I see that your parents really were just ahead of their time, because I see them all over Mayfair and don't even get me started on Hammersmith."

"I had that exact same thought when I first was brought to this time."

"Yes, the future is humbling, alright."

There was the sound of a phone, of someone receiving a text message.

We turned and it was Georgiana as she took out her phone.

"My sister has a mobile," her brother gasped.

"Yup."

"My sister is wearing 21st century apparel, and she is flipping open her mobile!"

"Yes, she has very much gone native modern-day Britain."

"Oh my god!" Georgiana exclaimed.

"What is it?" Colonel Fitzwilliam said. "And what is that?"

"It's called a mobile phone, my love," Kitty explained. "And I'll tell and show you later what it fully is. Now, what is it, Georgiana?"

"It's Tom. Tom Clarkson. He texted me back. You know what this means? It means that he is soft on me and he says that he wants to go out with me again."

"Go out with you again?" her brother asked. "What do you mean?"

Georgiana flinched and then she realized that she would have to go through all this again.

"I went out on a date with a man named Tom Clarkson, who is Mary's supervisor at her job. And now he wants to go out with me again."

"You're dating?"

"Yes."

Instinctively, her brother turned to my Mr. Darcy.

"She's dating?!"

"What?" Darcy scoffed. "Don't look at me, mate! It's not my bloody fault."

Chapter Sixteen

FAMILY

Eventually we had to return to Pemberly, because the house was too small to fit such a significant party, but there were also too many of us to drive in one car. Therefore, Elizabeth had to borrow a car from a group of friends while their children remained with their grandparents. So, in three cars, with us in my Mr. Darcy's van, then the rest in the other two sets, we had to travel to Pemberly.

Once we had arrived, we all dissembled, much to the joy of Earl and Lady Fitzwilliam.

"Oh, thank the lord for that," Earl Fitzwilliam cried. "While I enjoy the way the windows can roll down in those car-things, I confess that I infinitely prefer a carriage."

"And there is Pemberly." Lady Fitzwilliam sighed. "Thank goodness. It's nice to see that some things never change."

"And some things do," the other Mr. Darcy said. "There's indoor plumbing in there."

"Oh well, that's a plus, I admit," our mother acknowledged. "I always wanted a shower myself, and now we can have one."

"I always wondered why there were no shower baths in your houses when I was pushed into the past," my Mr. Darcy questioned. "Because they did exist."

"Oh, they only ever push out cold water, so we figured what was the point?" Mr. Bingley said, holding Jane's hand. He gazed out at the beautiful home. "Oh, Pemberly. Are you truth or are you fiction?"

"How poetic you are now, my love." Jane laughed and squeezed his hand.

"Well, I'm going to be a father now," he said, "so that pulls me quite out of fear and makes me romantic."

"I trust that you will settle in fine," Mr. Darcy said, looking to his family. "And I believe that I can leave you in the capable hands of my descendant."

"It's fine," my Darcy said. "I don't mind if you stay with us for a time, sir."

"Thank you, for I would like Lizzy and I to visit for a time. But I have to return home and spend more time with my children. I've been gone from their lives for months, and it is not fair to them."

"I see," I said. "Well, whenever you both want to return, we shall look forward to seeing you."

"I was wondering," Elizabeth said, "what if we introduce you to our children? Yes, you and he look like us, but if we just say that you are relatives who we look similar to, then they shall adjust."

I liked the idea. "You want us to meet them? Really?"

"Yes," her husband said. "I would like that. I really want them to meet you all. I don't know how much time you have to stay here, so I want them to know that they had family for a time."

"Then when you are ready, bring them to Pemberly," Earl Fitzwilliam said. "Forgive me, I'm not the master of the house, but I am the oldest, so that had best count for something. Yes, I would love to see my grand-nephews."

We all agreed to this, Georgiana hugged her brother once more and kissed her new 'sister' on the cheek.

"Come back soon."

"We shall."

"Oh and Mr. Darcy," my Mr. Darcy said, "there is the other thing."

"What other thing?"

"While you were gone, I took over your business. Or shall I say, I retook over my business."

"Oh, what did you do?"

"Nothing bad or anything. It is just that I missed it. You are returned now. Is there any way that I can still do it for a while, while you remain with you family, enjoying them?"

"Oh, I suppose that's fair."

"Thank you."

"Working so much becomes our identity, doesn't it?"

"Yes, it does."

We all watched them enter their cars, drive down the lane and disappear.

"Amazing," Mr. Bingley said. "My friend just drove off." He turned to my Mr. Darcy. "And yet I feel as if he never left."

"Oh, shut up, Bingley!" Darcy smiled, and then we all entered.

⚜

After doing our best to find clothes for our new arrivals, which was not difficult especially for Jane had purchased enough maternity clothes that she could spare to our mother and Lady Fitzwilliam. Darcy and Zach gave our father and the Earl some of their night clothes. Bingley, the Colonel and Lydia were our sizes pretty much, so we got to see them parade around in their new apparel, and it was quite an amusing sight.

"While I do not feel as regal-looking," Lady Fitzwilliam said, "I admit that I feel a great deal more comfortable."

"And I'm not in the mood to look a gift horse in the mouth," our father said, "for I'm in a place with a library that perhaps has two hundred more years of history."

"You don't even need to go that far," Mary said. "You can read books on one of our kindles."

"What's a kindle?"

"I'll explain it later."

"Oh, right."

"So, all this really did occur?" our mother acknowledged. "All that time, Lizzy, and you had actually fallen forward in time, then came back and had to keep it all quiet. I can't believe we all are now undergoing journeys that are this large."

"Neither can I," Kitty said, "but mama and papa, when you were taken. You weren't with us at Matlock."

"No, we weren't," our father said. "We honestly were at home, and we suddenly just got whisked away. Wait, do you think that our home is still out there now, still in Hertfordshire?"

"We know it is," Darcy replied.

"Yes, when I first came here," I said, "Mr. Darcy took me to Longbourn."

"And what was it like?" Lydia asked.

"It was under the ownership of one of Mr. Collins' descendants."

"Oh."

My family members looked at each other.

"And how does it look?" our mother asked us.

"From the outside, it looks the exact same. Of course, the inside has had some changes."

"Well, at least he didn't destroy the exterior," my mother said, dabbing at her eyes. "Odious man. And those Lucases! They are all for what they can get! Oh, excuse me, they *were* all for what they could get. Past tense."

"Is there any way, that we would be able to see it again?" Jane's voice was pensive.

"If you want, we could all visit it."

"I would like that," our father said. "It shall be very antagonizing, but I suppose it is cathartic to look at things that hurt. You will not be resolved until you feel the loss, sometimes."

"In a strange sort of way, that could make sense," Mary said. "But if we go, it still has to be a Thursday, because I work the other days."

"You work?" our mother gasped.

"Yes, I work at a bookstore."

Our mother covered her mouth.

"And you don't need to worry about it, Mrs. Bennet," Georgiana assured her, "for very soon, I shall also be looking for employment."

"Your brother will kill me if I let that happen," Darcy said.

"Luckily even I know that he doesn't really have much of a say in the matter," Georgiana assured him.

"My daughter works, huh?" our father asked. "Well, these really are strange times."

"Yes, they are," I said, "but around this time of year, and in this century, normalcy is not really in season."

"But what about Matlock?" Earl Fitzwilliam inquired. "What about our home?"

"Oh, you need not worry," Zach said. "It remains in the family and it still stands. We saw it."

He gave the story of when we visited, and when he had finished, it was now Colonel Fitzwilliam's turn to look flabbergasted.

"There really is a descendant of ours who looks like me?" he asked.

"Yes, he does," Kitty confirmed. "And he was very nice. Richard, you will like him."

"Like him? Then, you expect us to meet?"

"Well, I told him about you."

"You did?" He smiled, pleased. "Really?"

"Yes, I think he would like to meet you."

"The idea intimidates me somewhat, I confess. But I shall think on it some more."

ॐ

Soon it came time for dinner. As we went to eat, we noticed that our cook outdid herself and the meal was lovely. As we sat down, I had the good fortune to be seated next to Colonel Fitzwilliam, who had Kitty on the other side. While Kitty was preoccupied in talking to our mother, the Colonel turned to me.

"How are you, Colonel?" I asked warmly.

"I am well, thank you," he replied simply.

"Really?" I asked archly.

He chuckled. "Truly, I am fine."

"I am glad to hear it. And are we friends again?"

He smiled even more warmly.

"If you had chosen me, I never would have found your sister. So yes, we are fine."

"Thank you."

"But it's more than that, isn't it?"

Puzzled, I asked, "Pardon?"

"Well, now that I know the full story," he continued, looking at Darcy, "when I proposed, you were already in love with him, weren't you?"

"Yes, I was. Always had been."

"And when he came back from falling in the pond, that was not my cousin that returned, but rather it was him?"

"Yes."

"All that time I spent thinking that you threw me over for my cousin and his money, and it was not that way at all. Rather it was because he was the man who you have loved long before you ever met me."

"Long before I had even met your cousin as well. It was him only, Colonel, it had always been him who I cared for."

"It must have been hard for you."

"And it must have been hard for you as well."

"Yes, it was. So yes, we are friends."

Happier in the resolution that we had reached, we ate on in peace.

After the dinner, we all had rooms assigned to our family and then arranged another shopping day for them to get more clothes.

"I always wanted to visit Pemberly," our mother said, "I just had no idea I would have to fall through time two hundred years later to do it. Oh well, our bedroom is lovely!"

"And lovely is as lovely does," our father said, to which Darcy almost snorted.

"What is it this time?" I asked him. "Did they accidentally reference something?"

"Yes, they did. Absolutely amusing."

Once all were settled and knew where the nearest bathroom was, we dispersed for bed, and at last Darcy and I were allowed to return to our bedroom.

Once we got there, and he closed the door behind us, we smiled at each other.

"I've wanted you all day," I admitted.

"Me too," he ground out, pulling off his shirt. He took me to the bed and laid me down on it and pulled off all my clothes.

"Also, just to inform you, you are the handsomer Mr. Darcy."

He laughed. "You had better think so." Then he pulled off my underwear and we kissed passionately. With speed he kissed me down my neck then began to lick me along my breasts, sucking on my nipples deeply, then lowering his lips down along my stomach and at last wrapping my thighs around his neck and I felt his tongue and teeth tease me gently down there. He continued to tease me, and then he dove deeply into me and my back arched from all the sensations.

Although I was spent, he rolled me over, pulled me to my knees and kissed my bottom until I thought I would die from the pleasure. Just as quickly I became aroused once again.

I turned over, pushed him to the bed and jumped on top of him, lowering myself on his hips and we became one. As we rocked back and forth, my blood began to boil, and I felt the heavenly sparks of desire rushing through my veins. Soon, we were both filled with lovely relief, our breaths mingled. We lay there, holding each other.

"I confess," I said when I could catch my breath, "when I was speaking with the Colonel, I am surprised that you did not look jealous."

"Well, I realized something at last."

"What?"

"I realized that I ought to trust you always."

I smiled happily, for we had finally reached that point where all would be well.

Chapter Seventeen

LONGBOURN REVISITED

After a week, we were once more traveling to Hertfordshire, but therein lay the problem of transportation. Even Darcy's van could not fit us all, so Georgiana had to assist us.

"Tom has a license," she offered. "Can I ask him? It will be perfect because it shall make him feel more comfortable around you all, and then we could rent a van from a shop."

Since Darcy was the only one with a license, this plan was speedily accepted and to our surprise, Tom Clarkson was actually quite accepting of the plan.

"He gets to feel helpful," Darcy explained when Tom had come to the house to join us for the day. "That's what every man secretly wants the family of the girl he's dating to feel."

"You were lucky that I came with no parents at first, weren't you?" I asked him.

"Yes, I admit that I was. But you were even luckier."

I slanted him a glance. "Was I?"

"Yes, the mother of a son is always the scariest thing in the world."

"Do you think that your mother would not have liked me?"

"I was her only son. Of course she would not have liked you."

I pinched his cheek, we all assembled in the vans and then we were off, back to the place where all seemed to be the destination of: home.

To Longbourn once more.

Hours later, when we arrived, parked and exited, it felt not only like Deja vu, but it also felt even like it was on repeat. As we entered, the same Mr. Collins who had met Darcy and me before met us again, and for some reason, he even remembered us!

"I can't place my finger on it," he said, "but for some reason, you both just stick out in my memory more than any other."

"We'll take that as a great compliment."

He glanced at our entourage. "And you come bringing family with you."

We introduced him to the rest of our company, and he led us along the house once more.

"Oh, my goodness!" our mother cried in the parlor. "That's our table!"

"Pardon?" Mr. Collins asked.

"Oh," Tom Clarkson said, while he held Georgiana's hand, "do you have one just like it?"

"Yes, they do," Georgiana rushed out, looking at Mr. Collins. "I have seen it. It really does share an uncanny resemblance to a table in their living room."

"Yes, it does," Kitty also stressed, "doesn't it, Mama?"

"Yes, it does," our mother said, catching on. "It does indeed."

"This is actually an antique," Mr. Collins said. "And it is almost as old as the house itself."

"Yes, yes…ours is also quite the antique," our mother answered, quite wryly.

We walked onward, and our mother surprisingly grew pensive, thoughtful at everything that she saw. For indeed every now and again, something caught her eye here or there that was like it was in our time. Naturally it made her grow slightly wistful.

"Mama," Jane said, taking her hand as they dawdled behind the back of the group, "are you all right?"

"Nothing, it is just…it's one thing to know something will happen, and then to see it occur. I knew that we would lose Longbourn of course, but now I see it. This was our home, Jane. And now I see something hard, something painful."

"You see that eventually, everything ends?" Jane suggested.

"Yes," our mother confirmed, amazed that Jane could understand her in that moment. "Yes, and it makes me sad."

"Not everything, Mama," Jane assured her, squeezing her hand, "not everything ends."

Eventually Mr. Collins showed us to one of the bedrooms.

"Oh, you show bedrooms as well?" Lady Fitzwilliam asked, a little disgusted at the idea.

"Well, yes," Mr. Collins replied. "Naturally people wish to see how the bedroom of a regency home looks like."

"It's natural," I assured my parents and the earl and his wife. "All tours in homes do this nowadays."

"So, this is where the master and mistress of the home slept," our father said, knowing full well it was so, because this was our parents' bedroom. This was once his.

"Yes."

Lydia grimaced. "So then, this was where Mr. William Collins lived when he took over the house after he inherited it due to the entailment."

"Along with his wife," Mary added sadly, "Mrs. Charlotte Collins."

Mr. Collins looked confused by this.

"Beg your pardon, what do you mean?" he asked.

"Oh, that was the man's wife."

"No, it wasn't," he replied, to which I blinked in confusion.

"Yes, it is so," I stressed.

"No, it's not. His wife's maiden name was Miss Brenda Hamilton, who was a member of his congregation in Hunsford, where he had the living at the church."

We all looked at each other.

"What?" Kitty asked.

"Yes, he married a Miss Brenda Hamilton, and she became the mistress of the house when he inherited. Yet you in some ways are part correct. If I heard correctly from my father, who knew absolutely every bit of his family history from that time, before he got married to her, he was at one time engaged to a woman named Charlotte."

"One time?" I asked. "What happened?"

"Actually, I recall him being engaged twice before. The first time was to a sister in the Bennet family, whom he did not marry, due to some form of scandal."

I looked at Mary and Lydia, and they both looked down at their hands, one ashamed and the other heartbroken.

"After that fell through," Mr. Collins continued, "he proposed to a Hertfordshire lady named Charlotte, but a little while before the wedding, she called it off."

"What?" I gasped.

"Yes, we don't know what fully happened, but it was known that she broke it off, and ultimately refused him. It was said that she remained a maid her entire life and she spent much time away from home, in the county of Derbyshire, visiting friends."

History had been unwritten!

Charlotte had not married him! And six years ago his descendant told me something else, and now it had been undone, and he didn't even know it. He didn't even remember it.

Charlotte had revoked her acceptance of him, and the reason was as clear as day.

She often visited Derbyshire, and there would have been only one person who would have been there for her.

She had done it for me.

She sacrificed her future for me. And she even remained single, something she was trying to avoid, rather than continue to betray me and hurt Mary.

In that moment, my heart went out to her. There in the past, she still hated herself for what she had done, and still believed that I did not forgive her.

When I returned, that would be the first thing that I would do. In the end, she had remembered that we were friends, and that that came before anything else in that circumstance.

Standing there, I felt a hand close itself around mine and I saw that it was Darcy.

"I want to thank her." I sighed, emotion filling my eyes.

"Don't worry. You will."

Eventually the tour came to an end and it was time to depart.

"By all means," Mr. Collins said as we put on our coats, "if you have any more family, bring them by for another tour, because something about this place seems to draw you all back in."

We thanked him for his offer, and we walked to our cars.

"Well," our mother said, "I still hate the man he comes from, but at least his descendant turned out to be a very good man."

"Yes, so it would seem," our father replied, taking her hand. "A strange thing, it is."

"What, Mr. Bennet?"

"Well, all those years and you were afraid that we would lose Longbourn, and now I see why."

"Ah, now you see why I was always complaining?"

"Yes, well, it just took me being dead for two hundred years to get the message."

"Oh, we are not dead! Nonsense, we are just very much misplaced."

"How are you, Mary?" I asked her.

She shook her head sadly. "I spent all those months hating Charlotte, and she did the right thing in the end."

"Charlotte Lucas; the woman who keeps surprising us all."

We took one last look at Longbourn before we got into our cars and drove away.

Chapter Eighteen

FOOLS RUSH IN

As we drove back to Derbyshire, everyone else in the car had fallen asleep, while I sat in the passenger's seat and Darcy drove. I always did my best to stay awake when he had to drive a long time to keep him company, and this time, my mind was full of thought.

"What is on your mind?" Darcy asked me. "You have your pensive face on."

"It's in many places."

"You're thinking about your friend, Charlotte Lucas?"

"I was, but now I am not. I feel badly that she didn't get married due to her desire to make things up to me, for I was quite direct and short with her when she let me down."

"There's more to life than just getting married, even in that time period. She hurt your family, so don't feel bad. You had a right to confront her on that. And now she has made it up to you. She has her goodness now. Don't take it from her by getting mad at yourself because you forced her to see what she was."

"You think so?" I asked, hopeful.

"I know so."

I stroked his knee. "Thanks, I needed to hear that."

"I had a feeling."

"But in truth, I was thinking about something else."

"What is that?"

"I don't know if you are ready, but would you be willing…again, only if you are ready, to get married here? In this time period?"

"Oh," was all he replied.

"I know that you and Caroline were engaged for years, but I don't have all the time in the world. I could be separated from you at any time, and the same goes with our family. I have the majority of my family present now, and who knows? Maybe in a month from now, they'll be taken away from us. Blimey, Time might even be harsh on us and send us to an entirely different time period that is foreign to us. We do not know if we have a tomorrow. So, let me be married to you while I can." When I thought on what I said, I chuckled sadly. "I think I am proposing to you. Dear me, I am rubbish at it."

Darcy squeezed my hand. "Once more, I had a woman propose to me. Well, I do see what you mean, and while my pride is a little wounded by the fact that you beat me to the punch, my vanity is quite stirred because I felt the compliment of it. Do you mind, I sort of want this to be as romantic as it can get?"

"Of course." I brought his hand to my lips and kissed it.

"Very well, here we go."

Mr. Darcy pulled over on the highway, on a side street, and the van behind us followed us as he parked.

"What is it?" Tom Clarkson asked as he pulled up behind us. "Is everything all right?"

"Yes," Georgiana also said, poking her head out of the passenger seat window. "Everything fine?"

"Oh, it's great," Darcy said. "Elizabeth is just going to propose to me, that's all. I'm happy you're all awake, because I think that we need an audience for this. In fact, everyone wake up!"

Georgiana stirred the people in the van to wake up, and everyone in our van did so as well.

"What is going on here?" Colonel Fitzwilliam asked. "Aren't we on the side of a road? What, did the wheel thing break down or something?"

"Oh, it's called a tire, my love," Kitty said sleepily, "and if it did, don't worry, because we have spares."

"No, the tires are fine," I said. "I am just going to propose to Mr. Darcy, and I suppose it would be nice if you were awake for it."

"What? Really?"

"What do you mean you are proposing to him?" our mother cried.

"And on the side of a road too?" Lady Fitzwilliam said. "Can't you at least wait till we get indoors?"

"No, I am afraid that it cannot be helped," I declared. "I cannot wait a moment longer. I must propose to him now."

"Mr. Darcy!" our mother bellowed. "You will propose to her now, before she gets a chance."

"I'm afraid that I cannot do that, Mrs. Bennet," Darcy replied. "Your daughter is quite adamant, and you know that there is no arguing with her when she is in such a state."

"Elizabeth," our father said, "in such a situation, even I have to agree with your mother now. My dear, it's nighttime, we are on a strange street and surely even this century has such a situation as highwaymen."

"Oh, don't listen to any of us, Lizzy," Lydia said, "and go on ahead."

"Lydia!" our mother cried.

"Mama, this is long overdue. So just let it happen."

They all hushed and turned to us.

"Mr. Darcy," I began, "forgive me now, but I do not have a ring."

"Neither do I, but don't worry, we can get them later," he answered smiling down at me.

"Good. And we will. Mr. Fitzwilliam Darcy, of Mayfair, London, and of the 21st century, will you marry me? Will you be my husband and make me the happiest of women? I will always love you. I will never betray you. I will stand by your side, for better and for worse. Even when you are wrong, I will defend you from the world. We shall walk together as partners, no matter what time does to us; we shall try and always find our way back to each other and be there when the other one finds their way home again."

"Upon my word," I heard Jane whisper to Mr. Bingley, "that was actually quite lovely."

"Shush!" Kitty hushed her.

I turned back to Mr. Darcy.

"Well?"

He smiled, raised out his arms, and I took his hands.

"Elizabeth Bennet," he replied, "of course I shall marry you. Of course, I love you as well, most ardently. In vain I once struggled, when I thought I could not have you, and it will not do. We have been tested by life and Time itself, and through it all, I stayed sane and content, because I knew that I would always find you again. And no matter how far we are forced from each other, I will always come back to you. I will never let you go.

And I will be your husband, you shall be my wife, and I shall have you beside me for as long as Time lets us and even then, I will still keep you in my heart."

"Oh, and that was just lovely as well," Georgiana said, taking Tom's hand.

"Did I just watch your brother get engaged by the side of a road?" Tom asked her lightly.

"Yes, you did."

"Bloody fantastic." His smile was joyous. Darcy raised me up and twirled me around.

"My daughter is getting married to Mr. Darcy," my mother cried. "Whichever one that he is!"

"Either way, I'm still rich enough, so there." Mr. Darcy laughed as I lowered myself down and kissed him.

"Yes, because it's clearly your wealth that I am marrying you for," I kidded.

"Woman, you just proposed to me on the side of a highway, at night, where it is dangerous. This will make a great story for the children."

"Yes, it will."

"Oh, they are already talking about children," Earl Fitzwilliam said, "amazing. And upon my word, this highway is quite dirty and noisy."

Darcy drew me closer and we kissed ever so passionately.

༺❀༻

Wise men often say that only fools rush in when it comes to love, but Darcy and I had all the history in the world to fall in love, now it only left us the time to rush into marriage, which we were actually quite willing to do.

We returned to Derbyshire and immediately applied to the nearest church for lessons to get married. Spending the next few weeks working up to it, all was falling into place as Mary continued to work, Georgiana got a job as an assistant in a library at Lambton, she continued to see Tom Clarkson, and they really did take to each other quite well. Jane continued to have her monthly check-ups, but all was fine.

Until Kitty and the Colonel demanded that they wanted to have a double wedding with us. At first Earl and Lady Fitzwilliam were upset by this because they very much wanted to have them married at Matlock in their own time. They lost the battle, for Kitty and Richard were adamant. It then became clear that Lydia and Zach also wanted to join our happy day, but in such a circumstance, his parents had quite won out, for with him being the heir of Matlock, naturally all the tenants on the estate had to see his marriage, or else it would not be considered valid to all back in 1812. With Kitty and the Colonel, it could easily be overlooked; therefore eventually we were able to join them.

During this time however, another happy concept arose. Colonel Fitzwilliam began to express a desire to know more about Darcy's marketing business. With each and every day that we remained in 2022, Colonel Fitzwilliam grew open to the change of vocations in the world. In this time, it was respectable to work and there were more job opportunities that were open to him as a common Englishman rather than a younger son to an Earl in our own time.

He often asked Darcy if he could train him in some way and perhaps he could even find a job in the marketing company somewhere, whether it be an assistant job, or simply being an errand boy of some kind. He assimilated quite well. With his child coming, Mr. Bingley had all the time in the world to dote and assist Jane, and he was even more joyous when the gender of the child was made apparent.

"It's a boy!" he cried when they returned from a check-up. "Jane and I are going to have a son!"

❧

The days leading up to our wedding were not without us making connections to the outside world, however. We invited Elizabeth and Mr. Darcy in London to our wedding, and they chose that to be the day that we were to meet their children at last, and we also visited Matlock again.

This time was even more amusing, because the younger son, Richard, was there to give us the tour again, and when he saw Colonel Fitzwilliam, he almost fell down the stairs.

"Told you I knew a person who looked just like you," Kitty said, nudging him gently.

Richard was dumbfounded. "Yes, you did. But I had no idea it would be to this shocking a degree."

"You and me both, mate," Colonel Fitzwilliam said.

For Earl and Lady Fitzwilliam, it was even more off-putting. There before them were two versions of their younger son, and they knew not what to make of it.

"So then," Earl Fitzwilliam said, "your name is Richard as well?"

"Yes, it is," Richard said, and then he turned to the colonel. "So you are Richard too?"

"Indeed, I am."

"Well, jeepers! This is too scary for words."

"Well, you're a handsome devil," Colonel Fitzwilliam said lightly.

"You too. I can even say that you are the first man who is as handsome as me. And you are his parents?"

"We are," Lady Fitzwilliam said. "And you, sir, are most extraordinary."

"I try to be, and I am happy that you have all come. It turns out that the Queen will visit Matlock. Since you all live at Pemberly, I was wondering if you would be amenable to me suggesting a visit there as well? I think that it would be nice to show the unity between the houses."

"An excellent thought," Earl Fitzwilliam said, happy to not only see that his descendant was a jovial man, had an artless manner, looked like his son, but also that the Queen of England was going to be visiting the estate.

"It makes him not afraid of mortality," Lady Fitzwilliam would confide in me later on. "Every man fears his life's work will get lost to time, so this was nice because it assured him that his name would always live on. Eternity, Elizabeth, it haunts even the humblest of men."

Once more we were shown around Matlock, and as we walked, Kitty had neared Richard while Colonel Fitzwilliam was distracted and they both began to speak.

"You seem to be quite attached to this double of mine," he noted. "Are you both family?"

"Oh, no," she corrected, "actually, he is my fiancé."

"He is?" Richard blurted out.

"Yes, he is. And we are to have a double wedding with my sister, Lizzy and Mr. Darcy. In truth, when I first met you, I was already engaged to him, so I could not help but finding you to be the most agreeable man I had ever met." She gave him a bright smile. "For you quite reminded me of him."

"Oh, and I had no idea."

"Of course not, for I did not wish to freak you out at the time. After all, what man wants to hear a woman say that she is engaged to his twin when they first meet?"

Richard chuckled nervously at this. "True."

Kitty continued to talk on, and Richard smiled through it, but I could tell that he was a little wistful, realizing that he never really had a chance.

"What a domino effect," I told Darcy. "But I suppose that it is better that he undergoes this now than later on."

"Yes, but this will be something that he shall always feel like got away from him. After all, when Kitty kisses the Colonel, it will feel like he is watching himself kiss her. How complicated."

"So it would seem."

As the tour came to an end, Richard saw us off to the front steps to Matlock.

"Well, for those who are new," he said, "I hope you enjoyed my family's home."

"But you do not live here anymore," Earl Fitzwilliam said. "I cannot comprehend it, for it is an exquisite home."

"Yes, and it's too much for one man, or two or three really," Richard replied. "Besides, my family is not like yours. You all seem to be quite attached, so very much liking to do things in groups. With our family, we can go a whole year without seeing each other and it feels like nothing really."

"Amazing," Lady Fitzwilliam said. "For you have the feel of a family man."

"Not much family to make me into that, I am afraid."

It was amazing to see him standing there, and so much revealing what most people spent their lives concealing; he was lonely. Richard Fitzwilliam was lonely.

"Well," Colonel Fitzwilliam said, "forgive me for being forward and presumptuous, but if you ever wish for company while you are here, we would like to become further acquainted with you."

"Yes," Lady Fitzwilliam said, "we should love to have you over for dinner, oh, but I should ask my nephew."

"It's fine, Aunt," Darcy said, "it's a marvelous idea."

"Yes, and we don't invite you out of politeness," I stressed, "or falseness. If you like, we would love for you to come and visit us for a dinner every now and again."

"Really?" Richard said, bashful. "That actually would be quite lovely. Thank you. I would like to visit Pemberly."

"Splendid."

After we said our last farewells, we then left, and Lady Fitzwilliam looked out of the window at him as he went back into Matlock.

"So that is our future? Our descendants no longer live there, and my son has his second self, he is a good man, and yet he is lonely. I could see it in his eyes, he is lonely."

"Yes, he is. His parents are passed away and he doesn't speak often with his brothers. Perhaps it is best that Time brought you here."

"What do you mean?"

"I'm beginning to assume that there are other factors. Perhaps you were not brought here for your own benefit. But rather you were brought for his. He doesn't have parents. Or much family. So, you came to give him a moment of that."

"Oh, a lovely theory then."

"That's the best that I can think of."

"A romantic idea."

☙❦❧

Richard Fitzwilliam—the modern one, had in fact just been remiss in familial ties. For in no more than a few days' time, we did invite him to dine with us, and he duly came. Seeing the twin of her second son in this new man, it left Lady Fitzwilliam's heart open to being very affectionate toward him, and the man appeared to really be a son who was in desperate need for a mother at moments.

He came back once a week for our Saturday night dinners, and while his initial feelings for Kitty could easily have led to tension in the group, he would prove to be more like the Colonel than just in face, but also in action. Where one door closed, another one surprisingly opened.

Since her coming to the future, Mary's outlook altered for the better, and where an outlook can change a disposition, it can also change ones looks. Her face and figure appeared much more pleasing because she was now in a place where she could look after herself very well, provide for herself and have her own identity. Back home she clung to whatever label she could, but since coming, she was able to define herself in ways that were not offered to her before.

That, mingled with an improvement of look, clothing and hairstyle, Mary proved that she had never really been the plain one at all. She simply had her own style of beauty that was not to the taste of our initial times.

Therefore, when Richard Fitzwilliam came to our dinners, he found himself gravitating toward the one single person in the room the most:

Mary. For often Tom came to eat with us as well, taking up Georgiana's attention.

Mary, happy to oblige and more open to lively discussion than before, enjoyed his company, and thus the Colonel's twin gradually began to shift his attention from Kitty to her older sister. She began to grow exponentially, and even could be seen asking for Kitty and Georgiana's advice on dresses to wear for when he would come.

Thus, Richard Fitzwilliam's company at Pemberly very soon became a fixed thing, and he prolonged his stay at Matlock, even when the Queen was unable to tour the house as planned, due to breaking her leg in a fall. Often, we visited Richard there, to keep him company as well, but he often preferred to visit us at Pemberly rather, and Mary and he clearly began to date without even knowing that they were dating.

What a circle it all was!

I was marrying Mr. Darcy.

Jane was married to his friend, or the friend of his ancestor who he had to pretend to be once.

Kitty was marrying his cousin, or the cousin of his ancestor who he had to pretend to be once.

Lydia would one day marry his other cousin, etc.

And now Mary fancied the descendant to his aunt and uncle, etc., who *was his actual cousin.*

All of us were beginning to find our fortunes in the Darcy, Bingley and Fitzwilliam men. Was that the fate of us Bennets? If they had been meant for us all along, then Time truly was to be thanked, and not despised.

◈◈◈

As Jane grew larger, the days leading to the double wedding grew shorter. Kitty and I got simple but lovely white gowns to which Kitty was actually upset that wedding gowns had to be white. Our sisters were our bridesmaids, and thus the day came at last, when in a small church in Derbyshire, our family was, along with Tom Clarkson, who was now Georgiana's official boyfriend, and Richard was there, alongside Mary whom he had just asked out on an official date no more than a week ago, and they had spent every day together since in that week.

Yet before the ceremony began, while we were all assembled in the back of the church preparation rooms, we were told of the arrivals from

London. Mr. Darcy, Elizabeth and their two children were there, and sitting in the pews.

The time for confrontation was finally present!

The revelation did not deter me at all, nor unnerve me as I stood up. My mother was looking at Kitty and me.

"I never thought all those months ago," she began, "that such a day as this would come. Of course, I never could have predicted the whole time travel part, but that is to be expected. Yet everything else that has happened. This moment is really going to happen? It almost makes me accept that we lost Longbourn. You both did me proud."

"Thank you, Mama," we both said, kissing her cheek.

"Lizzy," she continued, "I used to often criticize you and your wild ways, but now I see that it really was your nature that has made this all possible. Forgive me, my child. We parents can often be so very blind."

I patted her shoulder, happy to see the good mother that I knew had always been hidden deep within.

Eventually Kitty and I were placed behind our sisters in their bridesmaid dresses, and our father was placed in between us, his arms linked with ours.

"I..." he began, "I have a confession to make."

"What sort of confession?" Kitty asked.

"Remember how back in Longbourn, when your mother always kept encouraging me to visit every eligible gentleman who came into the neighborhood."

"How could we forget?" I laughed.

"And I never cared to listen."

"Don't worry," Kitty informed him, "we did not forget that either."

"Well, I know that it appeared as if I did that because I didn't care, but now, well, it is better that you know me. Kitty and Lizzy, I am happy that you are getting married, but the truth is that I did care. I just don't like change. I complained, joked and ridiculed, but I loved the five of you running about the house, making noise, laughing and coming home. I just did not really want it to change, that's all. And it's changing now, I am happy for you, but I really am so very frightened. A part of me shall always wonder what it would have been like if only things could have stayed the same. With us all at Longbourn, no entailment, but of course, those were the wishes of a blind old fool."

I looked at Kitty, and we both had tears in our eyes. "Oh, father..."

"I just figured that it is better that you all know me now. I did care. I did."

We squeezed his arms affectionately.

Kitty said, "Here at the beginning of all things, you let us in, and we got to know you after all. Thank you, Father."

I gave him a warm, rather wet smile. "I knew you could do it. I knew you would one day show your heart fully."

"Yes, well, today is that day, isn't it?"

The doors opened, the wedding march was struck up and there by the reverend at the altar, stood Mr. Darcy and the Colonel, wearing wedding tuxedos.

Kitty and I beheld them behind our bridesmaids, where Jane first walked down with Mr. Bingley, Georgiana walked down with Tom Clarkson, and Mary walked down with Richard Fitzwilliam, who, despite being new to our circle, was very much willing to accept the role of groomsman for a wedding. Yet then again, he was an Englishman; perhaps he was just too polite to reject the request.

"I only feel sorrow that our aunt and uncle could not be here," I acknowledged.

"Yes, poor Aunt and Uncle Gardiner," Kitty said. "We're going to have our work cut out for us when we have to explain this one to them."

As Mary and Richard walked down the aisle, Kitty chuckled.

"Ironic, isn't it?" she asked. "Mary of all people."

"Yup," our father noted. "Mary of all people. You both chose two identical strangers, who are not that strange to each other. I suppose the future did her good."

"Much good," I said. "All that time and it turned out that she just needed a job. And more time to grow."

"Yes, it appears very much so. I suppose I can forgive life now, for playing this dirty trick on us. It has all been very amusing. With such reality before me, I do not believe that I shall ever find much entertainment in a novel ever again."

At last all the bridesmaids walked down the aisle with the groomsmen, took their seats and then it came time for us to walk down. Not trusting ourselves in heels, Kitty and I wore flat shoes, so there was no worry as we walked gracefully down the aisle.

"I'm worried that I might cry," our father whispered. "Now isn't that strange?"

As we walked down the aisle, I turned and saw Elizabeth with her Mr.

Darcy, and their two children. Though they were both very young, they easily could see the physical resemblance between me and their mother. I smiled at the family and we continued to walk down the aisle, where our grooms were waiting for us.

Our father released our arms, sat down and Kitty and I stood beside our future husbands as the service began.

The reverend gave the traditional words for the ceremony, but luckily this was not going to be a long wedding, as no more than twenty minutes into the service, the rings were requested. Mr. Bingley handed the rings to Darcy and the Colonel, for he was both of their best man, the rings were exchanged and then at last, came the final words.

"Do you, Fitzwilliam Darcy, take this woman to be your lawfully wedded wife, to have and to hold, for richer or poorer, in sickness and in health, for as long as you both shall live?"

Darcy agreed. Then the reverend asked me, I agreed, then the question was directed to Kitty and the Colonel, where both agreed as well.

At last, he informed us that now the husbands shall be permitted to kiss the brides, and I turned to my new husband.

"It only took me two hundred years to find you," I whispered.

"And was it worth it?"

"Yes, it was."

"I quite agree, *Mrs. Darcy*."

We kissed, as did Kitty and the Colonel.

Kitty was now Mrs. Kitty Fitzwilliam, and I was now Mrs. Elizabeth Darcy.

Though I was not the first one, for the first woman who turned into Mrs. Elizabeth Darcy was sitting there with her husband, clapping for us all as we walked down the aisle.

❧❦❧

"A beautiful service," Elizabeth said to us as the reception was transferred to the ballroom of Pemberly. Our company was not large, but it was the small gathering of true and cherished friends and acquaintances that fully supported the match.

I put a hand over my heart and sighed. "Thank you. In truth, I wondered if this day would ever happen for me."

"I was the same way when I first met Mr. Darcy myself. I wondered if it could ever end in so happy a way."

"We both were fortunate, weren't we?"

"Yes, we were."

I looked on her, feeling an immense amount of sympathy.

"I know that you and I will never become close friends," I said, "but you really must believe me when I say this. Elizabeth, I am happy that I met you, and he loves you, so very much. You have nothing to ever fear from me."

"I know that now," she replied, "and I see that he just had a harder time letting go of the past, but once he did, he truly did learn to see me for who I was. And now may I introduce you to my children?"

"Yes, you may."

Elizabeth called to her Mr. Darcy, and they brought their children forward as my new husband stood by me.

"Cassandra and Henry," Elizabeth said, holding her children's hands, "these are my distant cousins, Lizzy and her husband, Fitz."

"Pleased to meet you both." I smiled at them, lowering myself down, and then I looked to Cassandra. "My, you have a lovely dress there."

"Thank you," Cassandra said, "I like pink."

"Yes, so do I. When I was your age, it was one of my favorite colors."

"I like green too."

"Me too. Though my second favorite when I was your age was yellow."

"I like yellow," Henry said.

"Good boy, and you, little sir, look just like your father."

I smiled up at Elizabeth's husband and he nodded.

"And he's tall for his age too," the other Mr. Darcy boasted.

"Lucky boy."

Cassandra opened her mouth and then closed it.

"Oh, what is it?" I asked invitingly.

"Why do you and my mommy look so much alike?"

"Oh." I halted, looking at her parents. "Well, you see, even though we are distant family, we just got lucky."

"You four look like you are all twins."

"I know! Amazing, isn't it?"

"Yes, it is!"

"Come, come!" Mr. Bingley said, standing up and tapping his glass, "since there are so many of us here, I have a great desire for a bit of a dance. We have a piano here, and a couple of musically inclined accomplished ladies. Is there any way that I can persuade you all to dance after a wedding?"

We all agreed to it, but Georgiana offered to play, because she knew that Tom would not know any of our dances. Mary offered to watch little Cassandra and Henry as well, due to Richard's inability to dance, while Elizabeth whispered conspiratorially.

"Darcy taught me all your dances," she said, "because I was always curious about your balls in your time."

Thus, all the couples lined up, including our parents and Earl and Lady Fitzwilliam and we began to dance as Georgiana played.

"Now I get to dance with you at Pemberly again." I looked up at my handsome husband.

He smiled down at me. "I know! I wondered if we would ever get the chance. By the way, I love you terribly."

"And I love you."

"You are smashing!"

"Oh, am I?" I smiled archly.

"Yes, and you know it, don't you?"

"Well, when you put it like that…"

We danced on and on, enjoying the pleasure of our company when all of a sudden, we heard a shout. All the dancing stopped, and we turned to see who it was.

Jane was standing there, completely white in the face and only then did I see why as my eyes travelled down her body, where the bottom of her dress was wet. Her water had broken.

"My baby," she cried, "my baby is coming."

Chapter Nineteen

THE REVELATION

With all speed, we rushed Jane to the hospital, where she was immediately taken to the maternity ward, where her doctor, Dr. Sadler, was called in for her labor. As she remained there, her contractions grew further apart, and there we all were, in our wedding attire, pacing back and forth.

"And I had her dancing." Mr. Bingley groaned, pacing back and forth as we sat in the waiting room, "I could have hurt her or the baby."

"Nonsense, Mr. Bingley," Elizabeth said, "when I was pregnant with Cassandra and Henry, I danced quite often and also swam, and it did not hurt either pregnancy."

"Right, sorry," he replied. "I am just so nervous."

"And luckily, Bingley, you have nothing to fear," the other Mr. Darcy, his foremost friend, assured him. "That is the great thing of this age. Rarely does a woman die giving birth. There are so many advancements, so many improvements on the delivery process, that Jane shall not even feel too much pain."

"Yes, they give you medication to dull the pain," My Mr. Darcy added. "Even when my mother gave birth to me in the 1980s, she had it easier as well."

"Well, something can be said for all the confusion that we had to experience through this all," Mr. Bingley said. "If falling into the future gave Jane a better chance of survival—"

He was interrupted when Dr. Sadler entered, dressed in his whole surgical attire and he headed straight for us.

"Dr. Sadler!" Mr. Bingley rushed to him, and we all followed suit. "Well, I confess that this is quicker than I expected."

"Oh, I am sad to say that Mrs. Bingley has not delivered yet," Dr. Sadler began, "but she is strong and healthy, and I just came to inform you of an impediment to your wife's delivery."

"An impediment?" our mother asked. "What? She is not going to die, is she?"

"Of course not, by no means," Dr. Sadler assured her. "But there has been a development, and there are now complications that we did not foresee. Your daughter, Mr. and Mrs. Bennet, your wife, Mr. Bingley was in the midst of labor, where her contractions were normal, but there were two sudden breaks in the delivery.

"To put it medically, your wife's cervix stopped dilating and the baby stopped moving down the birth canal. Right now we are attempting to stimulate contractions to get things moving again, but there is a chance that it shall not be."

"And what does that mean!" our mother cried, openly distressed.

"It means that she shall have to have a C-Section, doesn't it?" Elizabeth realized.

"A C-Section?" Lady Fitzwilliam asked, puzzled. "What is that?"

"It means Caesarean Section," Dr. Sadler explained. "It's the delivery of a baby through a surgical incision in the mother's abdomen and uterus, so think of it as us having to cut into the bottom of her stomach. In certain circumstances, a C-section is scheduled in advance. In others, it's done in response to an unforeseen complication, such as it is now."

"You're cutting into my wife's stomach?" Mr. Bingley asked, frightened. Our mother and Lady Fitzwilliam covered their mouths, but I had heard of such a process before, for when I babysat back when I first came to those times, Gemma's mother had delivered her daughter by C-section.

"Mr. Bingley," I comforted him, "believe me, it is very safe. Mother and father, Jane will be well."

"Yeah, she will," Dr. Sadler said. "Many women deliver their children by C-section nowadays and there is nothing to worry about. I just came out here to inform you in case we cannot stimulate the contractions. But as of right now, your son has stopped moving down the birth canal which means that he is not leaving her body. Therefore, a C-section is what I recommend and your wife, Mr. Bingley, has been informed of all this and she has of course given us her permission to do this."

"Right."

Another surgeon came out of the doors.

"Dr. Sadler?" she said.

"Coming," Dr. Sadler replied, then he excused himself. Despite all of our assurances, Mr. Bingley could not help but be worried, our mother was nervous, and our father was silent. Due to my knowledge, I was not, for I knew that Jane would be well, so I sat down next to Elizabeth and her Mr. Darcy.

"You had a C-section," I asked her.

"Yes. With Cassandra."

"Ah."

At first there was silence.

"When it had come, were you frightened?"

"Yes, I was."

I turned to Mr. Darcy.

"Were you scared?"

"Yes, I was as well," he replied simply. I turned away from them and looked down the lot of us and cast my eyes on my Darcy as he stood next to Mr. Bingley, patting his shoulder.

"You will be as well," Elizabeth answered my thoughts, "one day, when it's your turn, yes, you will be scared too."

"That's not all that I am worried about," I said.

"I know," she answered. "It's not your life that you fear, but it is his. You're afraid of something happening to you, and you leaving him behind."

"How could you tell?" I asked her, but then I turned to her Mr. Darcy. "Ah, it's what you felt?"

"Yes, it was. Both times."

"Was it?" Her Mr. Darcy asked.

"Yes, it was."

They took each other's hand and so I left them alone.

After another half an hour, a nurse emerged from the maternity wing and walked toward us. Recognizing her as the woman who called away Dr. Sadler, we all approached her eagerly and the news was quickly delivered.

She gave us a gentle smile. "The news is good. Mr. Bingley, your wife is healthy, strong and just resting a bit, and you now have a beautiful baby boy."

Mr. Bingley's expression was heartbreakingly lovely as he began to weep.

"I have a son," he laughed merrily. "Dear me! I have a son. Darcy, whichever one of you, I have a son!"

Both of our Mr. Darcys looked at each other awkwardly, not knowing which was allowed to hug Bingley first, so Elizabeth's husband hugged his friend first, and my Darcy waited patiently and then hugged him as well.

"I have a boy!" he cried, weeping with joy. "Upon my honor! I have a boy!"

"And I have a grandson," our mother cried. "I have a grandson! My dear Jane, always doing what is best for her family. For a woman always does her duty when she gives a man a son."

"And what does that say of you, my dear?" My father laughed.

"Truly, Mama," Mary declared, "you surely know that a woman cannot choose what comes out of her."

"Oh, I suppose that is true, for it wasn't my fault," our mother cried. "No it was not my fault at all. But Jane has a son, an heir to Netherfield Park. Delightful."

"Can I see my wife?" Mr. Bingley pleaded.

"Yes, in just a few minutes, for she has to be cleaned up and relax for a moment, while your child is being cleaned. We'll come and get you in a few minutes so that you can all see her."

She was about to excuse herself when I had a fleeting revelation that I wished to address before she walked away.

"Nurse," I called to her. She turned around and faced me as I lowered my voice. "I just have a question."

"Yes?"

"When my sister's cervix stopped dilating and the baby wouldn't move, if we had not been lucky, and by that I mean, if we had not had any means of her getting a C-section, could my sister have ever been in any danger? This is just so that I understand the situation. Without the modern conveniences, could my sister have died?"

"Well, I see no reason to consider the matter in such a light."

"I just need to know. Say that we were not fortunate, and we had been born in a time where there were no such advancements in medicine, could my sister have died?"

The nurse scratched her neck as she explained.

"Well, since this is purely an academic discussion, a practiced physician could have reached in and tried to pull out the baby, whereas the baby could easily have passed away, or survived somehow, but there is the chance—that yes, she could have died."

"Thank you for telling me."

She nodded and then left.

Now it all came clear, now came the revelation.

I turned to the rest of our company, still in our wedding attire, and spoke before I could even think.

"This was not about us," I pointed out, looking at my Mr. Darcy. "This time, I mean. This was about her."

"Lizzy?" my Mr. Darcy asked.

"This was about Jane. It was always about Jane. What I mean when I say that," I continued, "is that the first time that I fell through time, perhaps that may have been fate's way of fixing itself. It was my job to find you, and it was your ancestor's job to find Elizabeth over there, so yes it may have started out that way. But really, look at everything overall. It was more than that. It was always larger. If I had not fallen through time, I never would have learned that your ancestor would almost die. I would not have been able to save him. And if I had not fallen through time, you would have married Caroline Bingley. And I also would have not tried to stop Charlotte from marrying Mr. Collins, she would have made a mistake, Colonel Fitzwilliam never would have found Kitty, Lydia would have been forced to marry Mr. Wickham, she never would have found Zach, but one thing is certain: Jane, all along, was going to fall in love with you, Mr. Bingley, and she was always going to have problems with her first delivery. If remaining in her time, Jane would have died. All of this was about us, and our family as a whole, but it was also to make sure that Jane did not die."

Everyone was silent, except for Richard and Tom Clarkson.

"I'm sorry, buy what the bloody hell are you talking about?" Richard asked.

"Seriously," Tom replied. "I do not get it. And did you really just say that you fell through time?"

"I'll explain later, don't worry about it," Georgiana assured him.

"Really, we will," Mary also promised Richard, but I could not care for their confusion. All of this now had begun to weave itself in full, making the scene clear. I had my Mr. Darcy, the right one for me. And Jane would live. Jane would perhaps always live now.

Kitty laughed and clapped her hands together. "That was it! Time was really just working everything out. It was ending all mistakes, all mishaps."

"It was," Elizabeth confirmed. "Jane is safe."

"Yes," Mr. Bingley said on a shaky sigh, "my wife is safe."

"Really," Georgiana assured Tom, "I will explain this all later."

"Right." He clearly wasn't convinced.

Richard and Tom! Proper Englishmen; they were too polite to say that that they thought we sounded insane.

Eventually, we were able to see Jane, and we went into her delivery room to see her hair wet with sweat, her face joyful as she cradled her son in her arms. When we entered, she beheld us.

"He's beautiful, isn't he?" She glowed.

"Yes, he is!" we all cried as Mr. Bingley rushed forth.

"Charles, look at him!" Jane cried when he sat down beside her. "Isn't he gorgeous?"

"Oh he is going to be brilliant," Mr. Bingley cried happily.

"I think he looks like you."

"He has your eyes though. And that's what makes him brilliant."

As we stood there, my Mr. Darcy took my hand in his and we looked down at the scene while all surrounded the happy couple.

Darcy spoke. "Well now. All that time we spent, soul searching, looking for each other and falling over many things, and all that time, it was leading up to this."

"Yes, isn't it delightful?" I couldn't contain my grin.

"Yes, it very much is."

"My nephew's birthday is the same day as our wedding day."

"Yes, now that's a story."

"Yes, yes, it is."

Eventually words failed us as we just stood there in the doorway, watching the scene.

The perfect scene it was.

The very best of things.

"I can't wait to give him a sister or brother," Jane replied, to Mr. Bingley's amusement.

"It really is good to have them close together," Lady Fitzwilliam advised, "because they can play with each other."

"Now that I have one grandson," our mother stated, turning to Kitty and me, "you should not long be outrun by Jane. It is your duty to give the Colonel and Darcy a son as well."

Ah, Mama! Always thinking of one thing and one thing only.

Chapter Twenty

THE SPLIT

We all returned to Pemberly. Jane would be brought home the very next day. Due to all the events of the day, we were quite exhausted, and thankfully no one had to work the next day. Richard and Tom stayed over as well in some guest rooms and we spent the rest of the day watching a marathon of shows on the BBC. How fitting!

After we had just finished watching an episode of Doctor Who, 'Journey to the Centre of the Tardis', I looked around to see us all. We were practically all falling asleep and it somehow made me happy with how far we had come.

Earl and Lady Fitzwilliam, taken so far out of time, and they had coped so well with it.

My mother and father lived to see Longbourn lost, yes, but they had their grandson now, and it was brilliant.

Kitty turned into the ideal for the man whose heart I broke.

Lydia had Zachary and was to become the wife of an Earl. In fact, now that I thought on it, she had actually made the most eligible match in the end.

Jane was alive.

Mary and Georgiana each had a life, had a job, a future, and boyfriends.

And furthest away, sitting on the sofa was Elizabeth with her Mr. Darcy and her two children. She smiled at me as Cassandra lay asleep on her lap; I returned the smile. We now had the best of things; we were not just friends now, but we were comfortable around each other. That meant a lot.

I rested my head against Darcy's shoulder as we were the last two to fall asleep.

"You know," he said, looking at the television. "I used to hate this episode, but now I love it."

"Why did you hate it?"

"I suppose I wasn't watching it closely enough. Now I see the point."

"Time is put to rights again after going wrong in the worst sort of way," I finalized.

"Yes, precisely."

I looked around at our family and wished that we could spend our lives just being like that, being so united, so bonded through our experiences.

I wanted time to stand still at last.

To halt.

To give way.

And be simple.

But of course, that is not what it does. Nor shall it ever do. Time stands still for no one.

۞

The next day, Darcy and I drove to the hospital with Mr. Bingley and we picked up Jane, who was a little sad that her pregnancy overshadowed my happy day. We assured her that we were content of course, and she felt lighter as we took her home.

Once we got there, she was overjoyed to see everyone still there as she walked up to the house with us all, and Mr. Bingley was carrying their son.

"Jane, he is beautiful!" Kitty cried, looking down at the baby. "Oh, I am an aunt now!"

"Me too!" both Mary and Lydia said. "And now we have to think of a name."

"Personally," Lydia said, "I always liked the name Byron. It sounds so deep and unique."

"And it's the name of one of the most nefarious poets of our time," Mary said, then she smiled. "Though, I admit that his writing is now growing on me."

"I'm making her read him more." Richard smiled conspiratorially.

Mary lightly bumped his shoulder and gave him a warm smile. "Oh shut up, you."

"Give us more time," Jane said, "for I want to get to know our little boy before we name him, to get a feel for the perfect name. Is that agreeable to you, Mr. Bingley?"

"Yes, it very much is, my love."

We all began to walk inside.

And then we heard the chimes.

And bells.

The bells of a clock.

I felt my insides freeze over, wondering if I was the only one to hear it, but as I turned, I saw everyone look with worry, even Richard and Tom looked confused.

"Can anyone hear a clock?" Richard asked.

Mary said, "Yes. You hear it too? Oh, I am so glad."

"What is that?" Tom asked.

"It's Time," Georgiana explained. "Remember when I said that we would tell you. Well, you are about to be shown. Tom, the truth is, we fell through time."

"What?"

"They did," Elizabeth confirmed, holding Darcy's hand along with her children. "The clock chimes when you are about to be taken back or forward. Now Time calls for them all again."

The chimes of the clock grew louder and louder, but we did not move.

"I do not understand," Lydia said. "Why are we not moving?"

"I don't know," I said, but I was soon interrupted when a burst of light erupted from the side of us, air flowed around us to the point where our clothes were whipping in the breeze. We turned to the force of illumination and we saw a large source of pale blue light erupting nearby, casting its rays on us. From under the ground, water rose, and it began to wet our shoes, but it stayed shallow.

"What is that?" Cassandra cried, still holding on to her parents.

"Something new," her father said, cradling her close.

I stared into it, and took a few steps, but my Darcy grabbed my hand. As I watched, something about it connected within me and I understood what it was.

"It's Time," I concluded. "It's how we have been travelling all along. Now it's just being seen."

Nearby, Elizabeth took a few steps forward and stared into it.

"And yet it did not take us," she realized. "But it's waiting."

"Waiting for what?" Kitty cried.

"For us," I said, turning to them. "For us to make a choice of who stays versus who goes."

"What do you mean that we have to make a choice?" Georgiana blurted out. "We never had to before."

I did not know why Elizabeth and I were able to discern the meaning of everything, but it was not defined. It was only felt. I understood the intent of everything now, as if the message was as clear as day.

"Because now everything is put to rights. And it is time that we go back."

"No," Georgiana cried, taking Tom's hand. "I don't want to."

"Neither do I," Mary said, looking at Richard. "I've fought for so long to figure out who I am. I can't leave now, not when I have found it."

"Me neither," Georgiana declared, then she also looked at her brother, her real brother, and back at my Mr. Darcy. "You did a brilliant job of looking after me. I grew because of you. But now I have my life, and my brother back. I will not forsake it."

Her brother kissed her cheek. "Georgiana, thank you. And I cannot go back, for my life is here."

"But so is mine," my Mr. Darcy said. "This is the era I was raised in. I could not take your place, try as I might. And Pemberly in 1812 needs someone to look after it."

With a determined look, the other Mr. Darcy walked up to him and took his hand.

"You don't get it, do you? You don't see?"

"See what?"

"You already are the Master of Pemberly. You already took my place. It was you that history remembered. And it's you that she needs." He gestured toward me. "Just as my wife needs me. My children need me. My descendant, I am proud of you, and I need you now to be brave, braver than anyone. I need you to save me again. I need a past, to make sure that our family always survives, and I need you to be that past."

"How can I?" my husband cried. "I'm not you!"

Mr. Darcy rested his hands on my husband's shoulders.

"No, you're not. You're better than me."

Both men wept as they held each other, and Elizabeth and I watched as our husbands reached a new level of beauty in their pleas toward each other. For we knew, better than anyone, it was one of us that had to return to our time, for so much depended on one couple remaining in the past, or nothing would ever get started. All else was optional, but this was required. Just as Mr. Bingley and Jane had to return or there would be no master of Netherfield Park, no connection to continue.

How clear and painful it all was. I looked at Elizabeth as she held her children's hands, and both children looked frightened, and I knew the sacrifice we had to make. The future was beautiful, it was safe and there were more chances, but yes, the sacrifice had to come. I walked up to Mr. Darcy and took his hand.

"Look after my sister, would you," I said, "and your sister as well."

"I will." Mr. Darcy smiled down at me. "And thank you both."

"I'll do my best," my husband assured him.

"I know you will," Mr. Darcy replied. "Because you already have."

I walked over to Georgiana and Mary, and I wrapped my arms around them and squeezed tight

"I shall miss you both, and I love you both."

"We love you too," Mary and Georgiana said, returning the hug.

"And what about me?" Kitty asked behind us, so I turned to her. "Will you miss me as well, Lizzy?"

I read her expression and the way that she and the Colonel stood away from us, and it hurt me.

"No, not you too Kitty!" our mother cried.

"Yes," the Colonel said. "We are remaining as well."

Colonel Fitzwilliam's family all were in an uproar. His mother cried, his father roared, and Zach ordered him to come with us, but the Colonel was resolute.

"This is best," Colonel Fitzwilliam replied. "Don't you see? I love you all, and I will miss you, but Zachary, I have to think of my wife now, as you would. Mum and dad, you know my situation. If I go back, I have to go back into the army and fight. I might die and then leave Kitty a widow. But if I stay here, I can get a job in Darcy's company, I can provide for her. We can live a long life together. I have to think as a husband now. I can provide this way. And Darcy and Georgiana will be with me.

"And," here he looked at Richard as he stood next to Mary. "And we have family that clearly wants more family around him now. Mama and father, you made Matlock what it is today, but it's not meant for me at that time. But in this future, it can be. Please, I love you, but you know, in your heart, that this is best."

Lady Fitzwilliam wept uncontrollably, but even they had to accept this, for they saw the logic of it.

There were tears as we all hugged each other, and the split was dividing us already.

As for Tom and Richard, whatever reality they needed to prove our veracity came and they dealt with it very well as our emotions boiled over, forever presenting us with the same painful partings spoken over and over again.

Our mother had a hard time releasing Kitty and Mary as our father looked broken, realizing at the last minute just how much he cared about the daughters he ridiculed so very often. Yet with the lives they created, with the bonds that had been forged, Mary and Georgiana's place in time had quite changed, and Colonel Fitzwilliam had the right to choose life, to choose providing for any family he might have.

His parents hugged and kissed him as Zach clapped him on the shoulder and bade him good luck. Mr. Bingley hugged the other Mr. Darcy once more, professed that he would miss him and both friends had to part once more, both placing themselves on the opposite ends of time.

Yet the light called for us and we both felt as if the choice had to be made quickly as the light beckoned, demanded and ordered us. Time was drawing itself around us and the chimes of the clock once more grew louder.

Thus, with many backward glances, we all lined up and first our parents went into the doorway through time, then Earl and Lady Fitzwilliam, then they were followed by Jane and Mr. Bingley, carrying their son. Jane turned around once and shouted her love to Kitty, Mary and Georgiana, and then Lydia and Zachary followed after her. And last, hand in hand, my husband and I followed, and as we walked to the door, I turned to my family, mouthed my love for them and then looked at Elizabeth.

"I am glad that we met," she said.

"So am I," I agreed, then she disappeared as we stepped into the light.

Chapter Twenty-One

PROPER PLACE

To the proper place, or to the most proper place we could be, we had arrived. Appearing out of nowhere, we all were standing in the sitting room of Matlock, and what was even more amazing was that Lady Catherine was there, pacing back and forth, with Anne blowing her nose.

What was even more incredible was that she was wearing the exact same clothes that she had on when we first left, showing that we had returned on the exact same day as when we disappeared.

Yet when we all materialized in front of her, wearing modern day clothes, she gazed on us in wonder.

"What the devil happened?" she cried. "How did you do that? And where did you all go? One moment I am screaming at you for being engaged to my nephew, then you all disappear, and Darcy keeps going in and out and you are all here—and are those your parents, Miss Elizabeth, oh never mind! And why are you all wearing those clothes? And where is Colonel Fitzwilliam? Where is Georgiana? What witchcraft is at work here? And Mrs. Bingley, why do you have a baby in your arms?"

Seeing her standing there was no longer intimidating, but in fact, it was quite amusing. We had gone through so much that her complaints seemed so small, so minute, and she would never realize it.

"Well, sister," Earl Fitzwilliam said, "in truth, we fell through time pretty much, woke up in the year 2022, we were there for months, Jane and

Mr. Bingley had a son, your nephew is now married to Elizabeth here, there is nothing you can do about it, and my son will marry Lydia.

"And my other son bravely decided to stay in the future to provide for his wife, Kitty, and Georgiana and Mary are with her as well. And through it all, I have learned something; that you are wasting your time trying to change any of this."

Lady Catherine threw up her hands in shock.

"Are you all mad? Tell me the truth."

"Oh very well," I said. "While I despise you, you deserve that much."

We all sat down nonchalantly while Lady Catherine looked on me in shock and alarm.

"Lady Catherine, I hope you are prepared." I gave her a cynical smirk, for now I knew that she could not touch me and never could, so all was well, "For I can easily say this. It is a long story."

Epilogue

After being told the truth, Lady Catherine declared us all mad, but she could not speak of it, because this was family business and you did not expose such things. She returned to Rosings Park, despondent and with disappointed hopes, and Anne de Bourgh eventually could not have cared less.

Eventually Mr. Bingley and Jane found a home that was close to ours in Derbyshire while Lydia eventually did become the rightful mistress of Matlock, married to her beloved Zachary. Our parents returned to Longbourn, but they often visited us at Pemberly, where they were joined by my good friend, Charlotte Lucas. Indeed, she did not marry Mr. Collins and he would choose another. My parents now were resolved that they would one day lose Longbourn, but the warmth of knowing our future was secure was comfort enough.

As for me, Darcy and I settled at Pemberly, accepting our roles as master and mistress, finding the happiness in each other's company, so dependent we were on each other, not liking to be away from the other for long.

Yet the future still called out to us, in the deepest of our souls, and often we could be seen, looking out at the stars, questioning them with our eyes, wondering of the family we had in the future who we missed and loved, and wondering would we have to wait an eternity to see them again.

Yet Time was not our province, but rather it belonged to itself, and we only could be left to wonder at it, and marvel at all that had occurred, and do as so many others had done before us: hope, wish and dream—and then accept that the dream would never come true.

Yet that is the strange thing about Time, I suppose; anything can happen.

And anything did.

Time was its own master.

And Time does not stand still.

And sometimes, just sometimes, miracles can happen, again and again.

And it opens itself up and presents itself to us, showing itself for being our very best friend and ally.

We thought time had fixed us in such separate places forever.

But nothing ever fully ends, now does it?

And nor did our adventures.

We thought Time separated us fully at that point, and that was it.

Yet Time had a thing or two up its sleeve.

We thought we would never see our family again. The family who was separated from us by centuries.

Until the day that we did see them. Until the day that we, in the past, fell back into the future. And those, of the future, fell back into the past. We were separated most of our lives, but every now and again, Time was kind. Time gave us all...one moment more.

Every now and again, there are miracles. And when they come, I advise everyone to chase them. Don't question them, only chase them!

THE END

৩৵৩

Don't miss out on your next favorite book!

Join the Satin Romance mailing list
www.satinromance.com/mail.html

THANK YOU FOR READING

❦

Did you enjoy this book?

We invite you to leave a review at your favorite book site, such as Goodreads, Amazon, Barnes & Noble, etc.

DID YOU KNOW THAT LEAVING A REVIEW...

- Helps other readers find books they may enjoy.
- Gives you a chance to let your voice be heard.
- Gives authors recognition for their hard work.
- Doesn't have to be long. A sentence or two about why you liked the book will do.

About the Author

Ney Mitch has been a long-standing Jane Austen enthusiast, having written forty novels that were inspired by her various works. Since stumbling on Miss Austen's books after graduating from college, she has always dabbled in Austen inspired literature, ranging from writing works for teens to adults. Originally, her desire was to adapt Jane Austen's writing in a way to help young adults connect with her, however over time, she has spread her aims to other genres and styles. Having received her BA Degree at Desales University, she is a writer, both literary and dramatic, as well as being a Historic Reenactor.

 facebook.com/courtney.mitchell.589

twitter.com/CMMitchelPsyche

pinterest.com/shebaanna

Also by Ney Mitch

WITH SATIN ROMANCE

The Memory Series

Moments of Moments Past

Moments of Moments Present

Moments of Moments Future

Pride & Prejudice Reimaginings

Rapture & Rebellion

Fortune & Misfortune

Desire & Destiny